CAMP CREEPY

Also in the Sinister Summer series

Wretched Waterpark

Vampiric Vacation

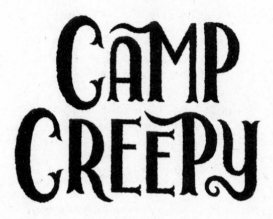

CAMP CREEPY

The Sinister Summer Series

KIERSTEN WHITE

DELACORTE PRESS

Text copyright © 2023 by Kiersten Brazier
Jacket art copyright © 2023 by Hannah Peck

rhcbooks.com

Educators and librarians, for a variety of teaching tools, visit us at RHTeachersLibrarians.com

Library of Congress Cataloging-in-Publication Data
Names: White, Kiersten, author.
Title: Camp creepy / Kiersten White.
Description: First edition. | New York : Delacorte Press, [2023] | Series: The sinister summer series | Audience: Ages 8–12 years. | Summary: The Sinister-Winterbottoms, twins Alexander and Theo and their older sister Wil, find themselves at a mysterious summer camp where they meet other families whose parents are missing.
Identifiers: LCCN 2022002275 (print) | LCCN 2022002276 (ebook) | ISBN 978-0-593-37912-7 (hardcover) | ISBN 978-0-593-37913-4 (library binding) | ISBN 978-0-593-37914-1 (ebook) | ISBN 978-0-593-65026-4 (int'l. ed.)
Subjects: CYAC: Brothers and sisters—Fiction. | Twins—Fiction. | Camps—Fiction | Missing persons—Fiction. | Mystery and detective stories. | LCGFT: Detective and mystery fiction. | Novels.
Classification: LCC PZ7.W583764 Cap 2023 (print) | LCC PZ7.W583764 (ebook) | DDC [Fic]—dc23

Printed in the United States of America
10 9 8 7 6 5 4 3 2 1
First Edition

To the kids who sneak away to read:
Don't ever stop

When Alexander emerged from the lake, not at all upset about how many microbes and bacteria and brain-eating amoeba he might have let in through his nose and mouth, he grabbed a tie-dyed shirt. That was another weird thing. Not only was he not wearing swim goggles—he usually refused to put his head underwater without swim goggles—but also Alexander never swam without a shirt. He was too worried about sunburns and skin cancer. He used the shirt to wipe off his face before dropping it on the ground instead of folding it and setting it carefully on a rock so it wouldn't get dirty.

Several of the campers patted him on the shoulder, and he laughed and patted them back, a perfectly normal casual interaction that, for Alexander, was anything but normal.

"Alexander!" Theo shouted. He looked up at her and waved brightly before getting in line for the rope swing again. Even when Alexander liked something mildly exciting, he had to take a break to calm down and reset before he wanted to do it again.

Was this how he was snooping? Trying to blend in, to lull Quincy into complacency so he could get answers? It was a brilliant idea, but Theo didn't understand how Alexander was managing it. He was acting like a complete stranger.

Theo rushed over. "What are you doing?" she yelled up the ladder, where Alexander was halfway to the top.

"Going on the rope swing!" he answered.

"Why?"

"Because everyone else is!" He gave her a thumbs-up, and she couldn't believe he was only holding on to a ladder with one hand, instead of strangling it in a death grip. "Hey, you're late for your tie-dye session!"

Alexander was right. Theo was due at the tie-dye cabin, and if she didn't show up on time, the counselors would start paying more attention to her. Then how was she supposed to successfully snoop? Was Alexander trying to warn her that they were on to her? Is that why he was doing this?

"Be careful," she cautioned.

Alexander laughed. "I don't need to be careful. We're just having fun!"

What was happening here? Who was this stranger in place of her brother?

CHAPTER
ONE

The Sinister-Winterbottoms had a problem.

Well, they had several problems. Their parents had dropped them off with a previously unknown—and seriously weird—aunt in the middle of the night and then disappeared. Sixteen-year-old Wil, twelve-year-old Theo, and also twelve-year-old Alexander had not heard from their parents once since then, other than a frustratingly vague letter.

There was a man with small, mean eyes and a large, mean mustache who kept turning up where they didn't want him. Which, to be fair, was a long list of places. Basically everywhere imaginable was a place they didn't want to see Edgaren't. The only places they might be happy to see him were: behind bars, in a pit with un-climbable walls, or at the DMV, a terrible place adults went to be tormented.

They had first met Edgaren't and his large, mean mustache at Fathoms of Fun Waterpark, where he had tried to steal the whole park. Then again at the Sanguine Spa, where he succeeded in stealing a locked book with their name on it. *And* there was a chance Edgaren't had been intending to steal them as well.

Currently, they were on their way to a camp where he might be lurking, which had seemed important when they left. Track him down, get their book back, and find out why their former friend Quincy was helping him. Somehow, especially to Alexander, going where they knew Edgaren't might be didn't feel like the best idea now that it was actually happening.

But, even with this abundance of problems, there was one problem that was quickly leaping to the top of their already-high problem pile: Aunt Saffronia's car wasn't working. More specifically, it seemed to be . . . disappearing.

"This car wasn't a convertible when we got in, was it?" Theo stared upward in consternation, a word she liked because it was like confusion had populated an entire nation. There had definitely been a normal, solid car roof above them at the beginning of the drive. And now there was only sky.

"That's weird," Alexander said.

"Which part?" Theo answered, gesturing to everything around them.

"No wind."

He had a point. There was no breeze. It was like they were sealed in against the world. But the boundaries of that seal were dissolving. Even the windows seemed less solid than they had a few minutes before.

Theo was very brave—sometimes to the point of being reckless, though she was trying to be reckful whenever possible now—but she drew the line at speeding down a lonely, empty forest road in a car that wasn't sure whether or not it wanted to keep existing.

"It was *not* a convertible when we got in." Alexander was sure of it. He wouldn't have gotten into a convertible, worrying that there was no roof above him if the car were to flip or if an aggressive hawk were to take a liking to his hair. He had nice hair, always neatly parted and combed, and he could imagine exactly what it would feel like for a hawk to sink its greedy talons in.

Unlike his twin, he was not very brave, and never reckless or even reckful, preferring tremendous caution in all things. He was thoughtful and careful and deeply, deeply worried. As a default, but particularly at the current moment.

It had been bad enough heading toward a camp where Edgaren't might be waiting for them. Worse, too, that Alexander suspected it was the same camp he had seen a book about. A book entitled *A History of Summer Camps and the Unexplained Disappearances of Various Campers in the Mountainous Lake Regions*. Worst that they were doing it in a car that wasn't dependable.

Their dad knew a lot about mechanics on account of building battle robots in their garage all the time. He would agree that a dependable car had a reliable engine in good working order *and* a body that didn't disappear at random.

Alexander watched the mountainous landscape with dread, waiting for a lake to appear. He should have broken rules for once and aggressively borrowed that book from the Sanguine Spa library. At least then he'd know what they were getting into. Surely their friend Mina, who owned the spa now thanks to their help, wouldn't have held it against him.

Sometimes reading was a necessary survival skill. And Alexander really wanted to survive.

Wil should have had an opinion about the state of the car, but she was too busy staring at Rodrigo. Rodrigo, its case covered in shiny stickers, was her constant companion. But it was the shine of its screen that held a magnetic grip on both Wil's eyes and her brain.

"Here, twerp," she said, holding her hand out. "Let me be in charge of the keys to the books until we find them."

Alexander was more than happy to relinquish the ring of tiny keys he had gotten from Lucy's nest. Holding on to the keys meant being responsible for them, and even though he was the most responsible twelve-year-old possibly in existence, he didn't *want* to be responsible for something so important.

"About the car," he said, hoping Aunt Saffronia would reassure them. But instead, as though triggered by their doubts, the car drifted to a stop.

"What's wrong?" Alexander asked. They were surrounded by towering trees so green they were nearly black. The road beneath them was cracked with disuse. It didn't look like anyone was around for miles and miles.

Aunt Saffronia stayed in the driver's seat, gripping the steering wheel. "I can't go any further," she informed them.

"So the car *is* breaking." Theo was glad to have it confirmed, even if she had never heard of a car breaking down by slowly evaporating. It didn't seem like an overly car-ish thing to do. Then again, it was their father who was mechanically minded. So maybe he'd have an explanation, if he had bothered to stick with them this summer.

Theo glared out the window. But that wasn't quite right. She lifted her hand and held it straight through where the window no longer was. Theo glared out the empty space that wasn't a window anymore.

This was all their parents' fault, and she was mad at them for being gone. Being mad was easier than being worried about where they were, why they had gone, why they hadn't come back or even called. Why there had been a book with their family name on it at the Sanguine Spa's secret hidden library, and why a mean mustachioed man would want that book and the six others like it.

Alexander found it easy to be worried enough for the both of them, though. His worry was always generous that way. He was sure his mom could have reassured him, would have laughed and declared this all an adventure while passing out cookies she miraculously produced from her depthless purse. But she wasn't here, and unlike Theo, Alexander wasn't mad at all. He was just scared.

And he *really* wanted a book to distract himself with.

Two books, ideally. Both the Sinister family book and the book about camp disappearances.

Wil looked up, taking in their surroundings with a frown. If she noticed huge portions of the car were missing, she didn't indicate it. "Come on, Aunt Saff, we have to get there. I *need* to get those books."

But Aunt Saffronia didn't move. "We should go back to my dwelling. It's safe there. You'll be safe there. We can go other places, too. There is still much to be found. You've done well so far. Better than I hoped. Your parents wanted me to keep you in my sanctum—"

"What's a *sanctum*?" Theo asked.

Aunt Saffronia continued as though she hadn't heard. "—but I needed you to find what I could not. I fear they may have been right, though. Now that I have set you on this path, I cannot keep you safe. Not from what lies at the end of it. And we still do not have what we need."

She turned her head, much like an owl, pale eyes enormous as she looked at the antique timer on a brass chain around Theo's neck, and the magnifying glass Alexander hadn't realized he was clutching in his hand. Their friend Edgar at Fathoms of Fun had given Theo the stopwatch, and Alexander had found the magnifying glass attached to the locked Sinister family book.

They didn't know why Aunt Saffronia wanted them to find things. Theo hoped it was a secret theft ring, with Aunt Saffronia the devious mastermind. But it was hard to think of their aunt as a mastermind. She hardly seemed the type, with her vague statements in place of elaborately detailed heist plans, not to mention lack of understanding of things like phones or whether or not children needed to eat.

A shudder seemed to pass through Aunt Saffronia. Literally pass through her, like she was gelatin and someone had shaken her. Her enormous eyes didn't blink as she looked away from the children and down the road.

"Please," she whispered. "There is no welcome for me ahead. The sanctum. The sanctum is safe, a place where no one can reach me unless I wish to be reached. I should have kept you there all along, as your parents wished. We can go there." She pointed back where they had come from.

Alexander and Theo looked behind them, which was easy because now there wasn't a back windshield to the car, either. And there, shimmering in the distance, was . . .

Aunt Saffronia's house? It was hard to tell what it looked like. It was more the *idea* of a house.

Alexander could almost imagine himself in the kitchen with the black-and-white tile and the orange walls. Or sitting on his bed next to Theo's bed, the dark around them making the beds feel like little islands of safety in a cold, infinite void. He knew with absolute certainty that Edgaren't wouldn't find them there. That they would be safe. He had the opposite certainty about the camp they were headed to.

Wil wanted to go steal back the books, but Theo had a different reason. Quincy—Quincy, who had taught her to lasso; Quincy, who had seemed so cool; Quincy, who had been her friend—had betrayed them. Theo wanted to know why. Maybe then it would hurt less. Or maybe she just wanted to yell at Quincy and make sure Quincy hurt, too. Either way, the camp brochure was the only clue they had about where Edgaren't and Quincy had gone.

"Do you want to go back to Aunt Saffronia's house?" Theo asked. She didn't. But she wouldn't force Alexander. She'd done that in the past, and it never turned out well. She had learned to trust his caution as much as she trusted her own bravery. Theo lived with an entire hive of bees in her chest. Not literal bees—that would be a big problem indeed, and a modern medical mystery—but figurative bees, meaning the bees weren't real, but they were the best way to describe how Theo felt. How she had a hard time managing or even understanding her emotions a lot of the time.

When she was bored or agitated or angry or scared, the bees buzzed to life. And right now, they were swarming, demanding vengeance and buzzing for action. But Theo was working on controlling them. She could quiet them enough to let Alexander make the choice.

Alexander wasn't angry with Quincy, and he wasn't eager to do anything that would put them back on a path that would lead them to Edgaren't, but he did love mysteries. And, while he didn't love being *in* a mystery, he knew the only way out was to keep moving forward. Quitting in the middle of a mystery just meant he'd have those nagging questions forever, without any resolution.

He hoped—desperately—that at the end of this particular mystery, they'd find answers about where their parents had disappeared to. And he knew—sadly—that none of those answers were at Aunt Saffronia's strange but safe house.

"No," Alexander said. Just like that, the house he

thought he could maybe see dissolved like a mirage, or the roof of their car. Of those three, only mirages ought to disappear, but this being the weirdest summer ever, who was he to say that roofs of cars or mysterious houses shouldn't evaporate?

"You are determined, then," Aunt Saffronia said with a sigh, and she sounded far away even though she was sitting right in front of them.

"Yes," Wil answered.

"I can go no further." Aunt Saffronia removed her hands from the steering wheel.

"*Farther*," Alexander corrected her. *Farther* was the word for things that could be measured and quantified, like distances. *Further* was more for concepts or ideas that no ruler or yardstick could define. "The car is broken, so you can't go farther."

"No," Aunt Saffronia said somberly. "There is no welcome for me ahead, no strangeness to slip into, so I can go no further into danger with you."

Alexander really didn't like the sound of that, but Wil didn't seem to even hear it. She got out of the car, eyes still on her phone. "I can text Mina and Edgar, see if anyone can get us a ride the rest of the way."

Alexander and Theo got out, too, wanting to be free

of the mysteriously modifying car. Maybe Aunt Saffronia was a genius like their dad and had designed a car that could fold in on itself? That seemed . . . unlikely. Alexander couldn't shake the nagging fear that if he stayed in the car, he'd be the next part to disappear.

He dragged his suitcase out and handed Theo hers. They stood, backs to the great aqua beast of a car, and looked out into the woods. The woods didn't return their look, because they were woods and they didn't care about the plight of the Sinister-Winterbottoms. Theo and Alexander felt as small as two average-sized twelve-year-olds could.

"Will you at least come to check us in at the—" Alexander started, but when he turned around, Aunt Saffronia was *gone*.

CHAPTER
TWO

"Why didn't she say goodbye?" Alexander said at the same time Theo said, "How did she get away that fast?"

One second the car was behind them, and the next, it was gone. Like it had poofed out of existence. They hadn't heard the engine restarting, or the tires crunching on this old asphalt, or seen a giant aqua beast slowly turning around on a narrow road.

Wil wasn't puzzled, but only because she was too engrossed in her phone to notice Aunt Saffronia was gone. "Mina says she's busy. The spa is hopping now, like Fathoms of Fun."

That was nice, at least. The Sinister-Winterbottoms

might not be having ideal vacations, but they *had* helped people worth helping. Theo wished she could go back to the water park now that no one was mysteriously missing in the Cold, Unknowable Sea, and especially now that their chef had added churros to the menu. And Alexander would have very much liked an actual relaxing week at the Sanguine Spa, instead of the stressful one they'd had, which included fears of vampires, mysterious tunnels and bat-filled caves, and more Marshmallow Fluff than he ever wanted to consume.

"So we walk?" Theo looked doubtfully down the road ahead of them. There was only the empty stretch of it through the enormous trees. Nothing and no one else.

"We don't even know where we are or how far away the camp is." Alexander clutched his suitcase handle, an increasingly tight, sick feeling in his stomach. "And no one knows where we are. And—"

"Edgar's coming." Wil put a comforting hand on Alexander's shoulder. He appreciated it. It meant she heard him, which she usually didn't, and also understood how scared he was. Wil wasn't always there for them, but maybe she was trying harder, too. "My GPS wasn't working with Aunt Saffronia nearby, but now it is, so Edgar knows where to find us."

"Why wouldn't it work with Aunt Saffronia here?" Theo asked, puzzled.

"Oh, you know," Wil said, waving vaguely, eyes back on Rodrigo.

"If I knew, I wouldn't have asked." Theo scowled, but the scowl was wasted on Wil. Perhaps if Theo had a phone, she could have taken a selfie of the scowl and texted it to Wil. That was the only way to be certain it would be seen.

"How long until he gets here?" Alexander didn't like the idea of being out in the open like this once it got dark. The day was warm and quiet, the trees tall and dark, with no one around to hear if they needed help.

"Dunno. We're not exactly at a track-each-other's-location stage yet. You still have the camp info, right? Edgar's never heard of the place before."

Alexander pulled the neatly folded brochure out of his pocket. It had almost no text but was filled with glossy photos of a blue, blue lake; green, green trees; brown, brown lodges; and big, big smiles. "Camp Creek," Alexander said, handing it over and repeating the camp's slogan: "*The summer every child should have.*"

"How can they know that?" Theo picked up a rock and threw it. She was feeling hot and sullen, and her bees had nothing to do except buzz around annoyingly, reminding her of all the other feelings that she didn't want to feel. "It can't possibly be the best summer for *every* child."

Alexander knew Theo was grouchy and wanting to argue about something, so he turned to Wil.

"You said you'd tell us why you answered your phone as Wil-o'-the-Wisp, and how you knew about the Sinister book, and what it is, and what the others are. And I've been thinking. There was a Sinister book, a Blood book, and a Widow book. That's our family, Mina and Lucy's family, and Edgar's family. And Mina and Lucy's parents are gone, and Edgar said his dads dropped him off at the water park in a rush in the middle of the night, just like our parents dropped us off, and he hasn't heard from them since, just like we haven't heard from ours since. That's too much of a coincidence. Something bigger is going on here, isn't it?"

Wil looked up. She tugged on one of her many dark braids, her big brown eyes narrowing in thought. "You've been paying attention."

"I *always* pay attention," Alexander said, mildly insulted. And it was true. People who are anxious pay attention to everything, all the time. Sometimes he wished he could pay a little less attention, but his brain was forever gathering information, sorting it, looking for threats or danger or things to feel embarrassed about.

"He does," Theo agreed. She could only pay attention to things she was already interested in, but this conversation definitely qualified. "So. Give us answers."

"I promise I'm on the case. You two have to trust me."

Alexander and Theo each rolled their eyes. Though they were very different, there were some things about the twins that were exactly the same. The freckles on their noses. The way they reached for the other's hand when they were scared or nervous. Their fondness for creating new words to describe weird things, like cabana mausoleums or castle spas. And the way they rolled their eyes when their big sister insisted they trust her.

"We do trust you," Alexander said.

"We just don't *trust* you," Theo said. "Remember a few days ago when you nearly walked off a cliff and we had to save you?"

"Or at Fathoms of Fun when you told us you were going to Charlotte's for a sleepover but really you were breaking into the park and you got caught and we had to rescue you?"

"Or when you got turned into a vampire?"

"That last one never happened!" Wil shook her head, indignant.

Theo shrugged. "But it could have, and if it had, we

would have saved you. So don't ask us to trust you. Start trusting *us* and giving us answers."

Wil sighed, looking at each one of them. "But you're kids."

"We're twelve," Theo said, outraged. "We're barely kids."

"But you *should* be kids. I want you to have a good summer. A carefree summer."

"The summer every child should have?" Alexander asked.

"Yes!"

"Well, it's a little late for that." Theo folded her arms. "Answers."

Wil let out an annoyed growl. "Fine. I don't think Mom and Dad went on a vacation. I think they gave us to Aunt Saffronia for protection, and I think, just like Edgar's parents and Mina and Lucy's parents, they're connected to the seven families from the books. If I can figure out what the connection is, then I can figure out where they all went. And *then* I can find them."

"Find them makes it sound like you think . . . they're missing?" Alexander felt his throat tighten around a scared, painful lump.

"I didn't *say* they were missing. Just that we don't know where they are. But I can figure it out. I promise."

Wil pulled Theo and Alexander into a hug. "Trust me. I'm taking care of things. You two shouldn't worry."

Alexander appreciated the hug, but any kid who worries a lot can tell you the worst possible thing to hear is that they shouldn't worry. Being told not to worry about something was both insulting—as if he had a choice!— and also even more worrying—no one tells you not to worry about something if there isn't something worth worrying about.

"That still doesn't—" Theo started, but Wil's phone chimed and she let them go, all her attention back on Rodrigo.

"Pavlov's bell," Theo muttered.

"Is that the name of Wil's ringtone?" Alexander asked.

Theo laughed, shaking her head. "No, but it should be. Pavlov was a guy who did an experiment where he rang a bell every time he fed his dog. Eventually the dog was so used to it that all Pavlov had to do was ring the bell and the dog would instantly drool, ready to drop everything and eat."

"Wil doesn't exactly drool when her phone dings," Alexander said.

"No, but she's definitely trained to drop everything and look at it. It overrides her brain."

Alexander sighed. It was true. He didn't get jealous of Rodrigo like Theo, but it did make him feel lonely. Like Wil preferred her world inside the phone to the one with them, outside of it. With their parents gone, it was worse than ever.

"I wish I *could* stop worrying," Alexander said.

Theo picked up a pine cone and threw it, then picked up another of the same size and threw that one, trying to see if she could beat her own record. "I wish you could, too." Theo didn't say it meanly, she said it matter-of-factly. Because it was a fact that she wished he could stop worrying, both for Alexander's sake and her own. Alexander's life would be a lot simpler then, and selfishly, Theo knew her life would be more fun.

Take the water park, for example. Even after things had gone back to normal—or at least, as normal as things ever got in that Gothic weirdo park—Alexander still had barely gone on any slides. It would be awesome to have a twin more like herself, one who would adventure right at her side.

Theo picked up another pine cone but dropped it as a tremendous roar echoed through the trees, surrounding them.

CHAPTER
THREE

The roar got louder and closer.

"What kind of animal is that?" Theo shouted, her fists clenched. Well, one fist was clenched. The other hand had found Alexander's.

The roar popped and let out a loud series of sputters and bangs. Alexander instantly calmed, his emotions responding before his brain realized why he wasn't scared anymore. It was an engine, and he knew those noises from all his dad's work.

The source of the engine noise quickly revealed itself to be an ancient sparkly violet motorcycle with a sidecar, driven by none other than their friend Edgar.

He wore a helmet, goggles, and his customary three-piece suit, complete with a purple kerchief around his neck.

He skidded to a stop in front of them and pushed his goggles up onto his helmet with a smile. "Did someone need a ride?"

"How did you get here so fast?" Theo asked. She wasn't sure where they were, but it was definitely some distance from Fathoms of Fun, where Edgar worked as a lifeguard and shopkeeper. After all, they had left from the Sanguine Spa, not from the water park.

"I was already at the spa. I left to get here as soon as Wil texted me about the—"

Wil shook her head, giving Edgar the universally recognized symbol for *shut it*.

"—very exciting opportunity to check out a summer camp?" Edgar finished, which clearly was not what he'd started out saying. But once he said it, he decided he meant it. "Can I see the brochure?"

Alexander handed it over. Edgar examined it with a puzzled frown. He had nice brown skin and nice black hair, currently hidden beneath his nice violet helmet. Alexander and Theo liked him very much, but not as much or in the same way as they suspected Wil did. As if to confirm their suspicions, she had Rodrigo lowered so she could look at Edgar. She liked Edgar's face even more than Rodrigo's screen.

"Strange," Edgar said, handing back the brochure.

"Really? It seemed pretty normal," Alexander said. "Like, if someone told me to imagine the most typical summer camp for kids, this is exactly what I would picture."

"No, not the brochure itself. It's strange that I've never heard of Camp Creek. We trade brochures with all the summer vacation attractions in the entire region. The Sanguine Spa, Stein Manor Science Camp, Carney Island, you name it, we advertise for them and they advertise for us. Professional courtesy to help people find the more off-the-beaten-path destinations. But I've never heard of Camp Creek. We don't have a single one of their brochures."

Alexander had heard of Camp Creek. At least, he suspected he had, and he wished he hadn't. He kept wondering what was in that book about camp disappearances. Why were there so many books in his life now that he wanted to read but couldn't?

"Oh!" Edgar reached into a saddlebag hanging on the side of his motorcycle. "When I stopped at the Sanguine Spa and said I was coming to meet you, Mina asked me to deliver this." Edgar pulled out none other than the book Alexander was just wishing he had.

"Thank you!" Alexander snatched it, ready to sit on the ground and read it right now, even though nonfiction was more Theo's thing. But Alexander liked mysteries, and *A History of Summer Camps and the Unexplained Disappearances of Various Campers in the Mountainous Lake Regions* felt like a clue. But his plans to read on the side of the road were immediately foiled.

"Come on, no time to waste!" Wil handed Alexander and Theo two helmets. Alexander's was yellow with flames painted along the sides, and Theo's was decorated with several skulls sticking their tongues out.

Wil put on the last extra helmet, which was matching sparkly violet, then pointed to the sidecar. It clung onto the side of the motorcycle in a way that reminded Alexander of a nature show where a baby sloth clung to her mother as she walked around. It was a reasonable way to travel at sloth speed, which was no speed at all. *Not* a reasonable way to travel at motorcycle-speed.

"Can I drive?" Theo gazed at the handlebars of the motorcycle with eyes that glowed almost as intensely as the flames on Alexander's helmet.

"Absolutely not," Alexander said at the same time Edgar more politely said, "Perhaps when you're older."

With a grumbling sigh, Theo squished in next to Alexander in the sidecar. It was meant for one large adult *or* two small children *or* luggage, and while the twins were not large, they were also not small anymore *and* they had luggage. The fit was all elbows and knees and helmets bonking against each other and absolutely no room to hold out a book and read. Wil climbed onto the back of the motorcycle behind Edgar, and they took off.

Most of Alexander's fears were soon soothed. It turned out the motorcycle was mainly sound and only a little fury. It sputtered and growled and often let out aggressive bangs, which contradicted the barely-faster-than-a-sloth pace it was capable of. Alexander had never ridden his bicycle faster than this, but Theo certainly had, and she was disappointed with her first motorcycle adventure.

It was a long, bumpy, and unfortunately buggy ride. Theo quickly realized that Edgar wasn't wearing goggles for the sake of looking cool—and he did look cool, somehow, much as he had in his old-timey swim clothes and parasol, because Edgar had the fortunate knack of feeling confident and good in whatever he wore and therefore always *looking* confident and good—but rather he wore them for the sake of not having his eyeballs turn into swimming pools for gnats, or trampolines for flies, or any other sort of entertainment for a variety of flying creatures. Theo and Alexander ducked, trying their best to keep their eyes and teeth bug-free.

Soon the road grew steeper, stitching back and forth to work its way up a mountain. The trees around them were deeper and deeper green, clinging precariously to the side of the cliffs the road was carved out of. Alexander didn't like this road one bit, and Theo wished they were going down, not up, because that seemed like it would be much more fun. At last, they plateaued, and the view took Alexander's breath away. (Which wasn't that hard, since Alexander was already breathless with nerves about the safety of the road, the condition of the motorcycle, and the camp that awaited them.)

A mountain range stretched all around them, dark conifer groves with bursts of brighter, more temporary green deciduous trees. There were whole fields of yellow and pink and purple wildflowers, and somewhere nearby they could hear a swiftly tumbling river. It was beautiful. So beautiful even if their eyes weren't tearing up from the wind and the bugs, they might have been tearing up anyway.

"I wish Mom were here," Theo whispered. Their mom always helped Theo slow down, helped her see details. Took her on walks at night and showed her all the hidden treasures of the midnight world. Together, they scooped stray worms and snails to safety, looked for owls, and studied the stars.

"What?" Alexander shouted.

Theo wiped under her eyes and scowled. Maybe being alone this summer wasn't their parents' fault, or maybe it was. Either way, their parents weren't here, and Theo would rather be mad about it than sad about it. "Nothing!"

Edgar followed the road past several perfect meadows, through dappled sunlight filtering through the trees, and along a winding, winking creek. And then, out of nowhere, a gate appeared. Edgar skidded to a stop. The brakes squealed in protest, much like a mother sloth might if her baby pulled her fur too hard.

The Sinister-Winterbottoms had been to the strangest water park ever, where the cabanas were mausoleums, the slides were gargoyle tongues, and the wave pool was a cave that triggered existential terror. They had visited the Sanguine Spa, with its tunnels and caves and downright vampiric residents—both the bats and, possibly, Lucy herself—and the woods that felt like they would eat the children if they could. They had braced themselves for whatever was next, certain that they were ready for any menacing weirdness they would face.

But nothing had prepared them for what they were looking at right now.

CHAPTER
FOUR

"It's so—" Theo started.

"It's so—" Alexander continued.

"It's so normal," Wil finished with a frown. She took off her helmet, her braids still perfect and beautiful. Theo and Alexander took off their helmets, their hair definitely not perfect or beautiful. Theo's looked like small rodents had set up a series of nests in it, and Alexander's was slicked to his head like he had recently pulled it from a bucket of water.

But Wil was right. The gate was wide open, welcoming. The sign was exactly what someone might expect a summer camp sign to look like. It was made out of two logs on either side, with lovingly carved block letters

29

that said WELCOME TO CAMP CREEK across the top. Though the K looked less weathered than the other letters, like it had recently been replaced.

"Whoa." Theo pointed. Up ahead of them the dirt road led straight to a wooded lodge with a cheerful green roof. There were cabins, miniature versions of the lodge, dotted around it. Everything bordered a glassy, mirrorlike lake, which was broken up with bright red-and-yellow canoes. There were kids playing volleyball, lining up to climb onto a rope swing platform, and a group sitting in a circle around a firepit, bent over some sort of craft.

"I know the brochure said it was a summer camp, but I really didn't expect . . . a summer camp," Alexander said. Even with the ominously titled book clutched in his hands, nothing here looked menacing or scary or even weird.

Two teenagers, one with bright red hair and a pale white face and another with a bright red face and pale white hair, were walking down the road to greet them. They both wore wildly tie-dyed shirts. Now that Theo noticed it, every kid she could see was also in tie-dye. Hadn't Aunt Saffronia said something about that, right after they left the spa?

"Hi!" said the girl with bright red hair and a pale white face.

"Hello!" said the boy with a bright red face and pale white hair.

"Hi?" Wil eyed them dubiously before looking back down at her phone. She hadn't been able to use it the whole ride up here and was clearly in withdrawal. "We need to speak with whoever's in charge."

"Great!"

There was something strange about the two counselors. Theo couldn't put her finger on it, though. The counselors were watching them, beaming, smiles almost as bright as the tie-dye swirls. Edgar wheeled his motorcycle over to the side of the gate. Alexander and Theo stretched, grateful to be out of reach of each other's elbows and knees.

"Do we leave our suitcases here in case we need to make a fast getaway?" Theo asked.

"Or bring them with us so no one can take them?" Alexander looked around warily, expecting Edgaren't to pop out from behind a tree, his mustache having grown even larger and meaner.

"Just bring them," Wil said, waving at them to hurry up.

"Maybe this is why Aunt Saffronia didn't want us to come here," Alexander said as they followed Wil, Edgar, and the counselors down the dirt road toward the buildings.

"Why?" Theo asked.

"Because there's nothing creepy or weird or strange or mysterious."

"Yet," Theo said brightly.

"Yet," Alexander agreed glumly. Theo was right. The only reason they knew about this camp was because Edgaren't was somehow connected to it. And nothing he was connected to could be good. Alexander kept a tight grip on his book in one hand and his suitcase in the other, the magnifying glass a reassuring weight in his pocket. The dirt road was perfectly maintained, running along the lakeshore, which glinted beckoningly.

Alexander refused to be beckoned.

Theo kept her eyes out for any sign of Edgaren't or Quincy, but it was hard to be sure who she was seeing. The campers didn't all look the same—there was brown hair and blond hair and black hair, skins of all shades, different body types, but somehow the sheer overwhelming shock of so much tie-dye made it hard to distinguish any specific people. They all sort of swirled together.

Before she could get a better look at any of the groups, the counselors stopped.

"This is the main office!" the girl with bright red hair and a pale white face said, holding her hands up to gesture at a smaller building tucked into the trees behind the main lodge.

"It sure is!" the boy with a bright red face and pale white hair agreed, opening the door.

"Kiki at the front desk will help you!" the girl said, holding the door for them to all file past.

"She sure will!" the boy said.

"I sure will!" a voice behind the front desk said. A teenage girl sat there with perfect posture, staring straight at them with a bright smile and an even brighter tie-dyed shirt. Her hair was in a ponytail, just like the girl with bright red hair and a pale white face, but Kiki's hair was a normal brown, as was her face. The desk she sat at was empty except for a clipboard and a bulky desk telephone. Her hands were on the desk, holding a pen at the ready. "I'd love to help you!"

"What's that phone for?" Alexander asked.

"For emergencies!" Kiki said brightly.

"Can I have the phone number, then?" Anything that was in case of emergencies was a case Alexander wanted to be prepared for. Kiki nodded, wrote it on a slip of paper, and slid it over to him. Alexander studied the number, committing it to memory and hoping he'd never have to use it.

"We need to speak to whoever's in charge," Wil said. Edgar stood next to her, nodding. They both looked out of place, with Wil's ripped jeans, black shirt, and black boots, and Edgar's elegant three-piece suit.

"Oh, absolutely! You definitely do! You for sure need to speak to whoever's in charge, and I will make that happen! What are your names!"

"I'm Wil, this is Edgar, and that's Theo and Alexander—"

"Sinister-Winterbottom!" Kiki finished brightly. "Yes, you're right here on my list! You're late to check in!"

"I'm sorry," Alexander said, feeling panic rising.

"Oh, don't be sorry!" Kiki's smile never budged. "There's no reason to be sorry, no reason at all to worry! We'll get you sorted right away, get you settled and started on the summer every child should have!"

"Does everyone here say everything with an exclamation mark?" Theo whispered.

Alexander couldn't help smiling back at Kiki. For once when someone told him there was no reason to worry, he sort of believed her. She seemed so genuinely happy, so absolutely focused on him. So *normal*.

"We didn't register them for camp," Wil said, putting a hand on Alexander's shoulder. "We're here to talk to whoever's in charge."

"Right! Absolutely! But kids aren't allowed back in the office, and you've come all this way, so there's no reason not to let Theo and Alex spend—"

"Alexander," Theo and Wil corrected her at the same time, which was thoughtful of them, since Alexander hated to be called Alex almost as much as he hated the conflict and embarrassment of correcting people.

"Right! Absolutely! There's no reason not to let Theo and Alexander spend some time here! They're already checked in and everything!"

Edgar gave them a worried glance. Wil was staring at Rodrigo. "Is that okay with you twerps?" she asked. "We'll be out of here soon."

"Yeah," Theo said, because she needed to find Quincy before Wil found their books and they left this camp behind.

"I guess," Alexander said, because he didn't want to tell Wil the truth: he was scared of the bright, happy, normal camp outside. Not even because of Edgaren't. Or

35

at least not only because of Edgaren't. But Alexander was also scared because he didn't know what the rules were here. He might do something wrong. And everyone was already separated into groups, so he'd be barging in without knowing the dynamics. They probably already had their friends picked, too, and he'd be unwelcome even if they were nice about it. His stomach was tied in a tight, sick knot, imagining it all.

It was embarrassing to be afraid of so many things that other people didn't even think about, and he didn't want to admit he wasn't okay with spending a little time in this perfectly ordinary camp. It would humiliate him in front of Edgar, who was so cool, and Kiki, who was so happy, and . . . whoever the red-and-white teens were.

"Great!" Kiki stood, marking something down on her clipboard. "Heidi and Ricky will get you all taken care of! Have so much fun! Wil and Edgar, if you'll come with me!"

Theo and Alexander turned around as Wil and Edgar followed Kiki and her stream of happy chatter through a doorway. Heidi—the girl with bright red hair and a pale white face—and Ricky—the boy with a bright red face and pale white hair—beamed at them.

"This is going to be so much fun!" they said in unison, putting a hand on each twin's shoulder and marching them straight back out into the sunshine.

"Remember," Alexander whispered, watching the kids laughing and playing and splashing and crafting, "that Edgaren't signed us up, and if he wants us to be here, it can't be good."

"No matter what it looks like," Theo said, scowling longingly at the giant rope swing out into the lake, and the canoes, and the archery range, and the perfect cabins, and the firepits, and the games. Leave it to Edgaren't to ruin the best summer camp she'd ever seen.

CHAPTER
FIVE

"We'll give you a tour!" Counselor Heidi said, her bright red ponytail swinging with the bounce in her step as she led Theo and Alexander down a perfectly maintained path past the lodge.

"Yeah! We'll give you a tour!" Counselor Ricky echoed, his pale white hair almost glowing in the sunshine.

"But first, let's drop off your things!"

"We're not staying," Alexander said, tightening his grip on his suitcase and book.

"That's fine!" Heidi said. "But let's drop them off anyway so you don't have to carry them!"

"So you don't have to carry them!" Ricky agreed. "They look heavy!"

Theo and Alexander glanced at each other. Theo patted where the timer was worn around her neck, hidden beneath her shirt. Alexander patted his pocket, where his magnifying glass was safely tucked away. They were in silent agreement that those things were not leaving their possession.

Heidi beamed. "We'll put them in cabin—"

"Let me guess, thirteen?" Theo interrupted.

"No, silly!" Heidi said. "There's no cabin thirteen! All our cabins have names, not numbers! That cabin is Fun!" She pointed to a cabin. It was the same log construction as the lodge. With their wooden walls and cheery green roofs, the cabins looked like they belonged, like they were always meant to be in this part of the forest. They all had a huge screen door and a bunch of windows so that the interiors weren't dim or dreary. Peering inside as they passed, Theo and Alexander could make out bunk beds, all neatly made with tie-dyed bedspreads. And sure enough, in large letters on the front of the cabin was written *FUN!*

"That cabin is Games!" Ricky pointed to the next identical cabin, this time with *GAMES!* written on it.

And so on, past *SPORTS!* and *TEAMWORK!* down the line to *WELL-ORDERED ACTIVITIES!*, *BLENDING IN!*, *RESPECTING ADULTS!*, and *HEALTHY HABITS!*

"Is it just me," Theo said, leaning close to Alexander, "or did they run out of good cabin names? *Respecting Adults!* doesn't sound like quite as much fun as *Fun!*"

"And here we are! This is your cabin!" Heidi gestured proudly to the last identical cabin. This one had, in the same large, extremely excited letters, the words:

EVERYTHING GOOD AND NORMAL!

"We're in cabin . . . Everything Good and Normal?" Alexander asked.

"No, you're saying it wrong!" Ricky answered. "It's Everything Good and Normal!"

"That's what he said." Theo frowned.

"No! He said, 'Everything Good and Normal!' But without the exclamation mark at the end!"

Theo frowned harder. "But that's punctuation. You can't hear it."

"Yes! We can!" Heidi answered. "We want everything here to be an exclamation mark of fun! It's very important to Camp Creek that everyone is having an absolute exclamation mark of a perfect summer! The summer—"

"Every child should have!" Alexander finished, being sure to include the exclamation mark this time.

"Yes!" Heidi's eyes lit up, and she clapped in delight. "You're already fitting right in! You're going to have so much fun here!"

"But we're not staying," Theo said, deliberately leaving off the exclamation mark.

"But you're here now!" Ricky answered. "So let's have fun!"

"No," Alexander said. "Fun is the other cabin. Let's have everything good and normal!"

Heidi and Ricky both burst into laughter as bright as their hair and their shirts. "You're so funny!" Heidi said.

"I like you so much!" Ricky said.

"I'm so glad you're here!"

Even though it was overwhelming, Alexander couldn't help but smile a little at the absurd levels of enthusiasm coming from Heidi and Ricky. Maybe all camp counselors were like this. There was still something weird about them, though, something he couldn't quite put his finger on. And it wasn't just the excessive exclamations, or their seemingly boundless excitement.

It was . . .

"Eye contact!" Alexander shouted.

"Yeah!" Heidi agreed.

"Eye contact!" Ricky echoed, pumping a fist in the air.

"I don't know why we're shouting *eye contact*, but I love it!" Heidi grabbed Theo's suitcase, and Ricky took Alexander's, going inside the cabin.

Alexander put a hand on Theo's arm to hold her back. "Eye contact," he repeated. "That's what's weird. All the teen counselors here. None of them have phones out. They're all paying attention. To what's going on around them. And to us."

"You're right!" Theo said, then corrected herself. "You're right." The exclamation marks were contagious. "I wonder if they're not allowed to use them while they're on duty."

"Do you think that would stop Wil?"

"Oh, absolutely not. But Wil could never be a counselor here, because she only uses exclamation marks when she's angry."

"True." Alexander braced himself to walk into the cabin. Maybe Edgaren't was waiting in there for them. Maybe this was where the camp would reveal itself to be secretly terrible, or scary, or dangerous.

But as he passed through the screen door into the cheerful interior of the cabin, it was, once again, exactly what he'd expect a camp cabin to be. There were suitcases and duffel bags shoved under the beds, which were all made up with their tie-dyed blankets. There were also huge tie-dyed sheets tacked to the walls, and on them hung posters.

One poster declared *SPORTS ARE HEALTHY!* over a photo of several balls. It hung next to one of a sensible car with *ASPIRE TO NORMALCY* printed beneath it, which hung next to a poster of a kitten that said *COMFORT IN REALITY*, which hung next to a poster of two men in suits shaking hands and smiling over the words *BUSINESS AS USUAL*. And all of them were backed by swirling tie-dyed cloths, so that the posters themselves were hard to focus on. Almost like they were wriggling. Alexander found himself staring, unable to look away.

Theo snorted in laughter. "Who's your camp decorator?"

"It's so great in here!" Heidi said, patting a bed affectionately.

"This one's my favorite!" Ricky said, pointing to a poster of a child smiling that simply said *SMILING!* on it. It did make sense that it was Ricky's favorite, since they hadn't seen him do anything but smile so far.

"I keep trying to think of a nickname for this place," Alexander said. "Like our cabasoleum, or the caspatle."

"But everything here is named exactly what it is," Theo finished. "This cabin literally is everything good and normal."

"Hey," Alexander said, "what's the ideal Camp Creek counselor name?"

"Heidi!" Ricky said at the same time Heidi said, "Ricky!"

"Nope. It's Mark. Because he's always ready for an exclamation."

Heidi and Ricky's eyes widened, and then they both burst into laughter even louder than the tie-dye in the room. "Oh, wow! I'm so glad you're here!" Heidi said.

"We didn't even know we were missing you, but we sure were!" Ricky added.

Alexander felt his chest swell. It was nice to be appreciated. He liked it a lot. Theo rolled her eyes. She liked Alexander's punny jokes, but they weren't *that* funny.

"Okay! Now that we have your things put away, let's check out at what's on the schedule for Cabin Everything Good and Normal!" Heidi looked at a clipboard on the wall. "Oh! This is exciting!"

"Archery?" Theo asked, then, getting her hopes up even higher, "Or intro to lockpicking?"

Heidi laughed. "No, silly goose! Archery is in the afternoon! Every camper starts with active meditation!"

Theo took everything hopeful she might have thought about Camp Creek back. This camp was *definitely* evil. She had managed to avoid Quincy's active meditation sessions at the Sanguine Spa. Was it a coincidence that they had the same thing here? She shared a meaningful look with Alexander. He seemed puzzled, too. They hadn't actually done active meditation at the spa, so neither of them knew what it was.

"Maybe it's a common thing," he said.

"Maybe it's where Quincy is." Theo's expression was much like a cat waiting to pounce. "Let's go!" she said, adding an exclamation mark and making her voice high and excited. She was going to find Quincy and get her answers.

CHAPTER SIX

"Meditation time!" Heidi and Ricky high-fived each other, then led Theo and Alexander out of Everything Good and Normal!, turned right after Fun!, and went through the back entrance of the lodge.

It led to a small room, with the door to the rest of the lodge closed. Theo looked for mats or pillows, but there were only several desks, much like the ones from school, with a hard, uncomfortable chair attached. She hated those desks with a burning passion. They were so boring and so hard to fidget in. She couldn't even tip the chair back and balance, since it was attached to the desk.

There was no one inside the room, either, so no sign of Quincy. "Where's the meditation area?" Theo headed for the closed door.

"This is it!" Heidi said. "Pick any desk you want!"

Alexander shrugged at Theo's impatient exasperation. He didn't know what to think about any of this. He couldn't help but feel like something weird was happening, but also none of the weird things seemed *bad?* Heidi and Ricky were too enthusiastic, but it was nice enthusiastic, the kind that made him feel sorry he couldn't match their energy. But he wished he could. He wished he felt like everything was exclamation mark—worthy all the time.

He took a seat. Theo took the one next to him, wishing she had a pen to start carving something into the desk so at least she'd have a task for her twitchy hands.

"Close your eyes!" Ricky said.

Alexander closed his lightly, feeling vulnerable. Theo squeezed hers shut tightly, feeling annoyed. She waited impatiently for the counselors to walk her through a forest, or lead her along a beach, or whatever other meditation imagery they had in mind. She didn't have time for this nonsense. "I'm looking for my friend, her name is—"

"You're not looking for your friend! You're meditating!"

Ricky said. He was still using his usual extremely upbeat voice.

"Aren't meditations supposed to be quiet and soothing?" Alexander asked meekly, not wanting to contradict them but really wanting to get this right.

"Not active meditation!" Heidi answered, then continued. "You've just woken up! How exciting! A new day! You open your closet and pick out your absolute most favorite outfit! It's a T-shirt and jeans and the most popular tennis shoes at your school!"

"My favorite outfit is—" Theo interrupted, but Ricky cut her off.

"Now, you've put on your favorite outfit and tied your shoelaces just like everyone else does! You go to the kitchen and sit down to your absolute most favorite breakfast! It's cereal with the perfect amount of milk! Wow!"

Theo couldn't help but snort a laugh. She liked cereal as much as the next kid—though their parents only let them have the sugary kind as a treat—but she couldn't imagine sitting down to cereal and being like, *Wow! Cereal!* Which was fair. Cereal wasn't a *wow* type of food. Maybe if they had sat down to churro French toast, or s'more pancakes, or toad-in-the-hole. Theo had never had toad-in-the-hole, but the name made her certain it was a very special, very silly breakfast that would, indeed make her think, *Wow!*

Alexander had never had toad in the hole, either, but thanks to his love of the show *The Magnificent English Confectionary Challenge*, he knew exactly what it was and was planning on making it for Theo for their next birthday. Definitely a bigger *wow!* than a bowl of cereal.

Heidi chirped onward. "Your parents kiss you on top of the head and pack your absolute most favorite lunch of peanut butter and jelly, chips, an apple, and a low-sugar imitation juice! The kind in the shiny silver pouch! Then your parents go to work! Your father is in business, and your mother is in sales!"

"What does that even mean?" Alexander whispered. He didn't want to interrupt, but he was struggling. His mother had never made them peanut butter and jelly, and he didn't like those juice pouches. If it was his favorite lunch, it would be noodle soup in a thermos with some of his mom's cookies on the side. And his father definitely wasn't in business, and his mother definitely wasn't in sales.

Actually, now that he thought about it, he didn't really know what their jobs were. But they weren't business or sales. "Mom only works at night, right?" he whispered to Theo.

Ricky shushed him, and Alexander squeezed his eyes shut harder, trying to make up for interrupting. Ricky picked up where Heidi had left off. "You join your neighborhood friends outside! Look at them! You have so many friends! Wow! So many friends!"

Alexander frowned, trying not to open his eyes. He *didn't* have that many friends. He didn't like playing in large groups. He always preferred one or two good friends. Theo had a lot of playground friends she did wallyball with at recess and lunch, but neither of the twins had other kids over often. Their parents always said friendship wasn't a competition, and it was the quality, not the quantity, that mattered. But it didn't seem like this meditation agreed.

"You and your tons of friends ride your bikes, and then you play a sport!"

"Which one?" Theo asked, already pulling ahead of all the other imaginary kids in a bike race and then beating Edgar on his motorcycle, too, for good measure. She wanted to stay on her imaginary bike, but Ricky and Heidi told her to picture a sport now.

"It doesn't matter! Any sport! You follow all the rules and play a perfectly ordered match!"

"You look like you're picturing a great sport, Theo!" Heidi exclaimed.

Alexander tried not to slump in his desk. He couldn't think of any sport. They all stressed him out, what with trying to remember the rules, trying not to let his team down, worrying he'd mess up and be embarrassed and disappoint everyone around him. The only sports he was okay with were ones he did all by himself, like running. Did running count? He didn't want to interrupt again and ask.

Theo wasn't having a hard time. She grinned, eyes still closed. "I'm figuring out how to combine lassoing with lockpicking."

"Those aren't sports!" Ricky said. He still sounded like he was smiling.

Theo opened one eye. "Lassoing takes lots of coordination."

"I'm sure it does, but you can't exactly join the school lasso team! So, after you finish your sport—soccer, or basketball, or baseball, or tennis, or golf, something popular and common!—you go home and read a book!"

Alexander let out a sigh of relief. The rest of this had been difficult for him to imagine, but he could *definitely* picture curling up in his window seat with a good mystery.

"Not that book!" Ricky said.

Alexander peeled an eye open. Ricky was looking right at him, a worried expression on his face instead of a smile.

"How do you know what book I was reading?" Alexander asked.

Ricky's smile came back. "You should be reading an assigned book for school that every other child has been forced to read and talk about!"

"Okay?" Alexander frowned, closing his eyes and trying to think of a book like that. Theo called them sad-serious-regular books, and while they weren't necessarily bad, they always seemed to be about the exact same types of children and also weren't ever the stories that stuck deep in his heart.

Heidi clapped her hands together like a physical exclamation mark. "Great job! Holding on to that day, write a list of the top five ways to have a really normal summer vacation!" She gave them each a piece of paper and a pencil. The pencil was covered with smiley faces, and the paper was swirled colors, like it, too, had been tie-dyed.

"Do you mean a *fun* summer vacation?" Theo asked.

Heidi shook her head. "No! I mean a really regular, normal summer vacation! One that you can go back and tell all your friends about, and they'll have the same stories! The summer every child should have!"

Alexander had already written out his number one, which was graveyard scavenger hunt.

Ricky looked at what he had written and shook his head, laughing. "I don't know anyone who does scavenger hunts in graveyards! That's not really normal! Try again!"

Alexander loved the graveyard scavenger hunt. It had been so much fun, working together with his siblings to solve the clues. And it had been a way to connect with their family's history, looking at the names of the people who had come before them. He'd made up stories about all of them. Some of them he still remembered. But Ricky was right. It really wasn't normal, was it?

Did that mean it was bad? Or just not right for this activity? Alexander hated getting answers wrong. He could feel himself starting to sweat, his heart racing.

Heidi put a fresh sheet of paper on his desk, then squeezed his shoulder in a friendly, supportive way. "Try again!" she said, her tone chipper. "I know you can do this! You're a great kid, Alex, and we're so glad to have you at camp with us!"

"Alexander," Theo growled. Alexander shot her a look of misery. "Just make it up," she whispered. "Then we can get out of here and look for Quincy." Theo listed exactly the sports Ricky had already mentioned, even though the very idea of playing golf made her want to break something. It was probably best to keep Theo and golf clubs far away from each other.

Alexander's mind was blank. He always prepared for assignments and quizzes, and he felt like he was somehow failing this one. He was letting Ricky and Heidi down, when they'd only been nice to him. He ended up writing *Eat cereal* five times. It was the only thing he could think of.

"Great!" Heidi said, and she really sounded like she meant it. "I love cereal, too! Wait until you see the breakfast here! Dispensers of all the most popular kinds of cereal! Sometimes," she said, and her voice got quiet like a whisper, but still louder than Alexander had ever spoken in his life, "if I'm feeling really wild, I mix two types together!" She started laughing, and Ricky joined her.

Alexander and Theo didn't know whether they should laugh. Fortunately, they were saved from having to fake laugh by a bell ringing outside. But it wasn't a bell so much as a weirdly layered tone, sustained and hanging

on the air loud enough that it could be heard from anywhere in the camp.

Heidi and Ricky froze, their laughs cut off mid-giggle,
like someone had pushed pause on them. Their eyes went
far away and blank, and they stood, completely still, un-
moving and unblinking.

"What's happening?" Alexander whispered, reaching
for Theo's hand.

CHAPTER
SEVEN

The odd tone continued, as did Heidi and Ricky's frozen-smiled staring.

"Are they broken?" Alexander whispered.

Theo stood and waved her hand in front of their faces. At that same moment, the noise ended as abruptly as it had started. Heidi and Ricky continued laughing like they hadn't stopped.

"Mixing cereal!" Ricky said, shaking his head. "Oh, Heidi, you're wild!"

"I know! Hi, Theo!" Heidi said, noticing Theo standing right in front of their faces, her hand still in the air. "Okay! Now that we have active meditation done, let's get you going on some activities!"

"I want to meet the other campers," Theo said. "I think my friend Quincy is here. I'd love to see her." Theo's clenched fists contracted her fakely pleasant tone.

"Oh, sure! You'll meet all the other campers eventually! We have so much fun for you before you meet with the camp director to find out when you get to make your first shirts!"

"I remember making my first shirt!" Ricky said.

Heidi blinked, and for a moment, her smile dropped ever so slightly, and Alexander and Theo could swear she didn't talk with an exclamation mark but rather a question mark. "Do you?" she asked.

"Do I!" Ricky exclaimed, and Theo and Alexander couldn't tell whether he was answering the question or wondering the same thing, himself. "Let's go!"

Heidi's smile popped firmly back in place, and she rushed Theo and Alexander out the door. She pointed to a small shed with an open door. "There's the craft shed, where you can get supplies to make boondoggles!"

"What are boondoggles?" Alexander asked.

"Long strings of bright plastic that you weave together to form chains!"

"What for?" Theo asked. It sounded tedious and annoying, and she definitely wouldn't be doing it. But chains could be menacing, or a hint of danger. She and Alexander peered into the shed as they passed. It was exactly as promised, lined with shelves filled with bins of craft supplies, most of which were bright spools of plastic thread. Nothing threatening at all.

"Because boondoggles are so much fun to make! And then you can have one of these!" Heidi pulled out a large set of keys from her pocket, complete with a key chain that held not one, not two, but at least half a dozen boondoggles of eyeball-meltingly bright colors. Theo, however, only had eyes for such a large set of keys. She was pretty sure those keys could get her anywhere in camp. So far she hadn't encountered a locked door, but surely there was one somewhere.

She looked at Alexander to see if he was thinking the same thing, but he was staring at what *he* only had eyes for. Wide, terrified, pre–panic-attack eyes for the rope swing.

The swing was at the top of a wooden platform. Kids waited in a neat row, climbed a ladder to the top, grabbed the rope, and then swung out over the lake and released to splash down into the water.

"No," Alexander whispered, as a way to reassure himself that he didn't have to do that. But he still couldn't quite look away. It felt like if he stopped watching, hyper-alert, something terrible would happen. Someone would forget to let go of the rope and swing back, bashing their legs against the platform. Or someone would let go wrong and get rope burns on the way down. Or someone would have forgotten they couldn't swim and be left floundering in the middle of the water. Or—

"You can't swim right now because you haven't changed clothes!" Heidi turned Alexander away from his view of the lake and the rope swing. He let out a sigh of relief. They'd definitely be gone before they had time to change clothes, and it would be impractical to get clothes wet now, anyway, since they weren't staying.

"So we can't swim," he said happily.

"But you'll definitely want to later!" Ricky said.

"Wanna make a bet on that?" Theo asked. She missed Alexander's hurt look. Just because Alexander was scared of things and didn't want to do them didn't mean he didn't *want* to want to do them. He wished he could.

But Theo was too busy looking everywhere else to notice Alexander's expression. None of the kids on the platform were wearing a cowgirl hat with their hair in two long braids. No one here was wearing a cowgirl hat at all, and there were no signs of lassos. Maybe Quincy wasn't here yet. Maybe Edgaren't had taken a longer route, or stopped somewhere first, or wasn't coming here at all since he didn't have the Sinister-Winterbottoms.

"Can we go find Wil and Edgar?" Alexander asked. Now that he knew the lake was on the schedule if they changed their clothes, it felt imperative to make sure he wasn't able to change. *Imperative* was a word he liked the weight of, because it meant important and required at once. It was both important and required in Alexander's mind that he not set foot in that lake or on that ladder up to that terrible, dangerous swing.

"But I want to do some activities," Theo said, staring longingly at the rope swing. She knew she should focus on finding Quincy or go help Wil and Edgar with their job of finding out Edgaren't's connection to the camp, but it all looked so fun. Or rather, it all looked so fun! She dropped her voice so only Alexander heard. "Maybe we can be campers for the day. Snoop around."

Alexander didn't feel like anything here would be fun. Every single kid was participating in whatever their groups were doing. There weren't any odd duos lurking in the shade, no one skulking off with a book. So everyone would notice when he didn't participate, and being noticed like that was humiliating and scary.

It was clear that Camp Creek was not the camp for him. Even though he hadn't wanted to come here in the first place, even though he knew Edgaren't was going to bring them here so it couldn't possibly be good, it still made him sad, looking around and knowing he didn't belong. Everyone seemed to be having so much fun, and having the same kind of fun as each other. Alexander felt weird and lonely.

"Finding Wil and Edgar's not on the schedule!" Ricky said.

"So you're saying you won't let us?" Theo braced herself, ready to make a break for it in case Heidi and Ricky were secretly evil and working with Edgaren't.

"Of course we'll let you!" Heidi turned toward the office. "It's just not on the schedule, is all! So we'll have to make adjustments! But that's okay!" She walked inside and then walked right back out. "Great news! Wil and Edgar are still in a meeting with the camp director! So you have time for activities! And if you're only going to be here for a few hours, we'd better pack them all in!"

"Yes!" Theo agreed, throwing in an exclamation mark without even trying. Alexander dragged his feet on the dirt road as Heidi and Ricky took them to a small building next to the lake.

"Crafts?" he asked, hopeful.

"Canoes!" Heidi answered.

"Nothing at Camp Creek is more fun than paddling around on the lake!" Ricky gestured at the shining mass in front of them.

Heidi clapped her hands. "Everything is *equally* as fun as paddling around on the lake, though! So you can't go wrong at Camp Creek!"

"I'll wait here." Alexander stepped back into the shade of a tree.

"That's not on the schedule!" Heidi said. She pulled out a life jacket and was buckling Alexander into it before he could think of a good reason why he absolutely could not go out in a canoe.

"Come on," Theo said, practically begging. "We'll get a perfect view of the camp. We'll be able to spy out Quincy much more easily from the water."

"I don't think that's true," Alexander said, and he was right. On the lake, the water would be brilliant and shining with the sun's reflections, making the deeper shade beneath the looming trees harder to pierce. So it would be the opposite: everyone and anyone could see them, but they wouldn't see the watchers.

But Alexander was too terrified to come up with that argument. Ricky practically lifted him into a happy yellow canoe—it was literally *HAPPY,* the word painted across the side—and Alexander sat so fast and hard it hurt his bottom. Then Heidi had put an oar in his hands, Theo had climbed in the back, and they had been shoved out onto the water before Alexander could scream *stop.*

"Stop," he whimpered.

"It's okay." Theo paddled with strong, assertive strokes. "You're wearing a life jacket, and you're a strong swimmer. There's a lifeguard tower." She pointed at a chair set ten feet in the air, reachable by a ladder. A tie-dye-clad teen sat in it. If Alexander was capable of relief at the moment, he would have noted that the teen appeared to be absolutely vigilant, smiling and waving as she watched all the lake at once, never looking down at a phone or any other distraction.

But he wasn't capable of relief. He clutched his oar so hard his fingers hurt. He sat so straight and still his spine hurt. And he thought of so many ways this could all go terribly, disastrously wrong, his brain hurt.

Theo was having a great time. She paddled them around the lake, trying out all the different ways she could move or adjust the oar to get them to turn, or go faster, or stop quickly. If Alexander whimpered a bit, well, it was easy to ignore over the sound of water slapping the bottom of the canoe.

She was having so much fun, she almost forgot why they were here. A new group of campers lining up for a game on the shore reminded her. She glided past them, as close as she could get without beaching the canoe. But the blur of tie-dyed children made it impossible to pick out individuals. There were no cowboy hats, though, so Quincy couldn't be there.

"One more pass?" Theo asked, tipping her face to let the sun tickle her eyelids.

"I'm going to be sick," Alexander moaned.

"Right. Sorry." Sighing, Theo carefully and smoothly paddled them to the shack they had launched from. There was a similar one across the lake, and she wondered what it was for.

Ricky and Heidi were waiting. They hauled the canoe up onto the shore so that the twins' shoes would stay dry. If Alexander were capable of any thought other than how badly he wanted to be on dry land again, he would think how kind the two overly enthusiastic counselors were. But all he could do was make a mad dash for the road.

He wanted to sit. For a few hours. He'd go get the book Mina had sent him, and he'd find somewhere quiet and he'd read.

"Wait," Theo called, catching up to him and grabbing his arm. "We need to do more activities."

"We don't need to. And I don't *want* to!" Alexander hadn't realized he was yelling until all the happy chatter around them instantly died. He turned slowly and saw that every single eye—counselors and campers alike—was on him. Every face puzzled and alarmed.

"You don't *want* to?" a boy asked, his lip trembling.

"How is that even possible?" a girl asked, looking at Heidi and Ricky for answers.

"Everyone wants to have fun at Camp Creek!" Heidi said, wringing her hands, smile still firmly in place.

"You're right," a calm, smooth voice answered. "I'll take it from here."

CHAPTER
EIGHT

The woman was tall and thin like a pine tree, but unlike a pine tree, she was swathed in brilliant tie-dye. Her hair was wrapped in tie-dye, too, all of which made her face peering out startlingly bland. It didn't match the vibrancy of her clothes at all. It was a face like a bowl of plain oatmeal in the middle of a table of birthday cupcakes.

"Hello," she said, her voice so smooth and unremarkable it was also like that bowl of oatmeal. Free of lumps but also flavor. "I'm Dr. Jay. I run this camp."

"Where are Wil and Edgar?"

"They asked to see my records, so they're looking through them right now. Very unusual teens." Dr. Jay looked down at Theo and Alexander, blinking slowly. "What would you like to do while you're here with us?"

"Everything," Theo blurted.

"Nothing," Alexander whispered.

"Hmm. I see. What do you like to do?" She turned to Alexander.

"Read," he said. "Mysteries, mostly."

"You like mysteries." Dr. Jay's face betrayed no emotion. "I have a mystery for you. There is a camper who's—"

"Missing?" Alexander gasped. He had been worried about exactly this. With all the trees, and the remote location, and the title of his book!

"No," Dr. Jay said, shaking her head slowly. "A camper who's refusing to join group activities. He's difficult to find. Perhaps, since you also seem disinclined to participate at the moment, you could explore the camp and find him. I'd like to talk to him and ask him what I can do to help him be happier here. He's my nephew, you see, and ever since his father left, things have been . . . difficult for him."

"Oh." That was not at all what Alexander had been expecting. But it suited their purposes exactly. He could snoop with permission and avoid all the activities. "I'd really like that."

"Excellent. Thank you. I'm sure if you end up staying with us, you'll find other activities you like as well."

"Doubtful," Theo muttered.

"No, I said I'm sure because I can guarantee it," Dr. Jay said. She turned her nearly colorless gaze on Theo. "And you would like to do everything?"

"Yes. All the activities. With all the kids. Every single one here."

"Well then." Dr. Jay gestured at the camp. "This is the summer every child should have. So go have it."

"We should stay together," Alexander said.

Theo grimaced. She didn't want to stay together. She wanted to go shoot arrows and jump off a rope swing.

"Everyone in the camp is together," Dr. Jay said. "We're all one." She nodded at the brilliantly happy tie-dye everyone wore. She had a point.

"Divide and conquer?" Theo suggested hopefully.

Alexander knew it wasn't the best idea. He knew that Theo was only suggesting it so she could go and have fun without him. And he was absolutely miserable knowing it. He didn't want to be a drag, to hold her back. "Don't forget why we're here," he cautioned instead of saying what he wanted to: that they should stick together no matter what.

"I won't!" Theo skipped back toward Heidi and Ricky. She wouldn't admit that Alexander was right. She told herself—lied to herself—that she was making the best choice. That she was doing this to look for Quincy and to get answers about the camp.

But as arrow after arrow thunked into the target, getting her ever closer to a bull's-eye, and as she strapped into a harness to climb a huge climbing wall up, up, up into the trees, and as she whooped in delight going down the zip line through those trees, Theo didn't find any answers.

She wasn't looking.

Alexander was, though. He wandered through the cabins, peering under beds. Nothing was strange or scary. He wandered along the camp paths, not straying from them or going into the trees, keeping a sharp eye out for any loners like him. But there was no one.

He was the only kid in the whole camp not having fun.

Leaning against the wall of Everything Good and Normal!, he stared out at the lake and all the kids there and tried his best not to cry.

He missed his parents, and he missed his bedroom, and he missed his books, and he missed getting to decide what he wanted to do and when he wanted to do it. But he also wished, desperately, that he was the type of kid who could come to a camp like this and have fun. It wasn't fair. Any of it. He kicked the wall of the cabin.

"Hey, watch it!" the wall said.

CHAPTER
NINE

Alexander jumped, squeaking in surprise and fright.
Had the wall of the cabin just gotten mad at him?
"I'm sorry?" he said timidly.

"You should be," the voice grumbled. It wasn't coming from the wall at all. It was coming from beneath it.

Alexander crouched down. The cabins were all built to sit two feet up from the ground. Probably to protect them in case the lake ever flooded. The water would run under the cabins, instead of through them. Thinking of the lake flooding, all the water rushing to get him since he wouldn't go to it, made Alexander want to climb the nearest tree.

But that would be scary for a myriad of other reasons.

Who would want to go under a cabin, anyway? The only things that could fit in those crawl spaces were things that creeped and crawled and were, by their very nature, creepy-crawly. Who knew how many legs belonging to how few creatures were under there? Why did the number of legs attached to a creature increase the level of creepiness so much? It wasn't addition, it was multiplication. Four legs on one animal? Four units of scariness. (Alexander found most animals mildly frightening.) But add four more? It wasn't eight units of scariness then; it was at least sixteen. If not more.

He shook his head, trying to focus. Now was not the time to try to calculate how scary various creatures were. The creature he was talking to had only two legs and thus was only a little scary.

Though the area under the cabins was blocked off with thin strips of wood, it was clear a human someone had figured out how to access it. "Are you— Who are you?" Alexander asked.

"Leave me alone!" the voice snapped. "Go cry somewhere else! This is my spot."

Alexander stood, hurt. He was pretty sure he had found who he was looking for. But this kid was a jerk. He wanted nothing to do with him. If Dr. Jay hoped to figure out how to help the cabin creeper have a good summer, she had a big job in front of her.

But . . . the cabin creeper wasn't the only kid not having fun, skulking around here instead of doing group activities.

Was Alexander just as bad?

"Dr. Jay wants to see you," he said, trying to sound like he hadn't been about to cry. It was a cruel fact that being called a crybaby triggered hurt tears in most kids. Just like being told you have a bad temper makes you mad. Somehow, shouting *I don't have a bad temper!* never seemed to prove your point.

"I'll bet she does! She wants to make me have fun!"

"So?" Alexander asked.

"So I don't want to! She can make everyone else, but she won't make me!"

"No one can *make* you have fun," Alexander said, and he wished it wasn't true. He wished she could make him have fun, could make him fit in here. Instead of giving him this task. Everyone else was playing and enjoying themselves, and he was being called a crybaby by someone burrowing under a building.

"*She* can," the cabin creeper hissed. "And when you're

out there having fun and I'm down here in the dark, I won't help you."

Alexander suppressed a shiver at the other kid's tone. He changed his mind about his creepiness math. This kid might only have two legs, but he was definitely as creepy as something with four, six, or maybe even eight.

"Why would I need your help if I'm having fun?" Alexander demanded. He wanted to have fun. Didn't every kid? Well, every kid except this one. Alexander didn't want to be like him. "I'm going to tell her where you're hiding. It's not safe down there."

"It's not safe *anywhere*. You'll see, crybaby!"

"Joke's on you, because I already see that." Alexander hurried down the path, glad he at least had answers for Dr. Jay. She seemed nice enough, and she'd be glad to know where her unpleasant nephew was.

"Alexander!" Theo shouted above him. He looked up in time to see her go whizzing by overhead. His own stomach dropped in sympathetic horror, watching her sail down the zip line. He wanted to ask what the tensile strength of the line was, how it was secured on either end, when the last time the harness had been checked, whether the helmet Theo wore was the appropriate size, and other extremely pressing questions. But Ricky jogged up to him, grinning, and before Alexander could ask anything, Ricky was leading him to the zip line.

Heidi was helping Theo unbuckle from the harness. "Oh, hi! Your turn!"

"Absolutely not," Alexander said.

"That's not why I brought him!" Ricky said. "You two wanted to see Wil and Edgar!"

"Yes!" Alexander was relieved. "And I also have something to tell Dr. Jay."

"Oh. Right. Wil and Edgar." Theo looked longingly back at the zip line. "Sure."

"Well, come on, then!" Heidi's bright red ponytail bounced along in front of them, leading the way. Theo already missed the archery range, and the canoes, and the zip line, and all the jumping and climbing and rope swinging and swimming she hadn't been able to do yet.

It wasn't fair that all these kids got to have fun, while they had to track down a big, mean mustache.

Alexander and Theo, both feeling that things were deeply unfair, walked right past Heidi as she stopped by a group of camp counselors playing an elaborate hand-clapping game. Alexander hated those games. He got so nervous that he inevitably messed up, even though he could do it all perfectly when he was alone.

Heidi laughed from behind them. "Hey! I thought you wanted to see Wil and Edgar!"

The twins turned around, frowning. That was when they realized two of the camp counselors they had walked past, two of the camp counselors wearing tie-dye and beaming and slapping their thighs, then their shoulders, then clapping their hands in a complicated rhythm, two of the camp counselors blending in perfectly with all the other camp counselors were, in fact, the two people they were going to see.

"What happened to you?" Theo whispered, horrified.

CHAPTER
TEN

Wil was wearing tie-dye.

Gone was her black shirt and her ripped jeans and her black boots. Her new shirt was swirling rainbow, her shorts were khaki, and her tennis shoes matched the shoes of everyone around her. Even her long braids were pulled back into a perky ponytail.

Edgar wasn't in his three-piece suit anymore. Theo and Alexander had been wrong about him after all. Edgar didn't make *everything* he wore look cool. He looked downright dorky in his khaki shorts, blue-and-yellow-dyed shirt, and lanyard complete with whistle. But he was smiling like he didn't have a care in the world, and seemed totally ordinary, like he had never carried a parasol for shade while wearing an old-timey bathing suit at a Gothic water park.

"Oh, hi!" Edgar said, waving.

"That's my brother and sister!" Wil said, pointing in rhythm to the clapping game.

"Her hands are empty." Alexander elbowed Theo hard in the side to point it out.

"What are you doing?" Theo demanded.

"Since you two are already registered as campers, they were nice enough to let us sign on to be counselors!" Wil did a quick spin, slapping her palms against the palms of the counselor next to her. How she had learned this game so fast, Alexander and Theo couldn't say. "So we get to stay here with you! It's great!"

"Yeah!" Edgar bent over and slapped his palms on the ground as Wil and the counselor on Edgar's other side high-fived where his head had been. "We have the whole week together at Camp Creek! It's going to be so much fun!"

Both Wil and Edgar jumped in the air, lifting their knees high as the counselors next to them clapped under their airborne, identical tennis-shoe-clad feet.

Then the whole group finished with simultaneous high fives, shouting, "Camp Creek!" Wil and Edgar laughed, hugging and high-fiving everyone around them to congratulate each other on a flawlessly performed, bafflingly complex clapping game.

"So . . . we're staying?" Alexander asked. The lake sparkled with menace in the distance, seeming to grow larger until it swallowed everything and it was all he could see.

"Sure are!" Wil said. "So have fun! We'll be by tomorrow to help you with tie-dyeing! Don't go without us!"

Alexander didn't know which was more disconcerting: seeing Wil play a group game while wearing bright colors, seeing Wil without Rodrigo, or seeing Wil making such intense eye contact with him. Was she trying to communicate something? He had no idea. He wasn't used to Wil making eye contact at all, so any version of it was unusual.

Theo frowned, trying to figure out the same thing, but Wil and Edgar were both beaming at her. "We *need* to stay?" she asked, trying to get answers without asking specific questions in front of so many other people.

"Absolutely!" Wil said at the same time Edgar said, "Definitely!"

Theo shrugged. It was good enough for her. Obviously

Wil and Edgar hadn't found any hint of the books yet. Maybe this was part of their plan to find it. Or maybe, she thought, hopeful, this camp was actually safe and they decided to take advantage of the fact that they already had spots here.

They seemed like they were having fun, too, even if it was a type of fun Theo would never have guessed Wil might be into. Theo was glad to stay because she still hadn't seen any sign of Quincy. Maybe her former friend would come later in the week. She was sure they could handle whatever Camp Creek threw at them in the meantime, since it mostly seemed to be throwing overly enthusiastic but nice camp counselors and activities that Theo had no problem doing.

If anything, she was excited. She could have *so much fun* while waiting to find Quincy.

"Where's Rodrigo?" Alexander, who shared none of Theo's excitement, asked Wil. Whether Quincy came later or not, he didn't care. He didn't even care if Edgaren't was lurking around here somewhere. The whole camp was so intimidating, so scary, such a reminder of how weird he was for thinking a camp like this was intimidating and scary. He didn't want to spend the rest of the day here, much less a whole week.

"Oh, everyone checks in their electronics! They're all locked away where we won't be distracted! It's wonderful!"

Did Wil's eye twitch as she said that, or was Alexander imagining it? Maybe he was, because this whole conversation felt imaginary. There was no way Wil would declare it *wonderful* to be separated from her beloved phone.

"Can we talk?" Alexander asked. Wil was acting weird. Or normal, but that was weird for Wil.

"It's not on the schedule!" Wil chirped. "But I'll see you around, and I can't wait to take you to your tie-dye session tomorrow! Don't go without me! It'll be great!"

She and Edgar moved as one with the other counselors, away from Theo and Alexander.

"Come on! Dinnertime!" Heidi said, putting a hand on each twin's shoulder and guiding them toward a path through the woods.

"Dinnertime is the best!" Ricky said.

"Yeah! So is swimming time!"

"Yeah! So is game time!"

"Yeah! So is pottery time!"

"Yeah! So is bed time!"

Ricky and Heidi continued their chatter, listing what

Alexander could only assume was literally every single thing they did at camp. Heidi and Ricky were not picky.

"But I have to tell Dr. Jay I found her nephew," Alexander said.

"Oh, Henry!" Heidi chirped. "He's always creeping around somewhere!"

"So, wait, you know? She didn't actually need me to find him?"

"We all look out for him! It's on the schedule permanently, though no one has ever caught him! Sometimes as a group activity we play Spot the Skulker!"

"It's the best!" Ricky laughed, adding it to the list of all the best things.

Alexander shrunk in on himself. It didn't sound like the best. Compared to all the other kids here, he was definitely more a Henry than a Theo, and it hurt his feelings preemptively, imagining what game they might play based around him.

"I'll tell Dr. Jay you spotted him, though! Great job! It's a point for Cabin Everything Good and Normal!"

"You get points for finding him?" Theo perked up. She was very competitive.

"Yes! We get points for everything! Everyone combines them, so the whole camp has over a million now!"

"Oh." Theo perked down. If everyone was winning, then no one was.

Alexander was trying to be brave. He really was. He was trying to be okay with the idea of the week stretching ahead of them. Trusting that if Wil and Edgar wanted them to stay here, then it was safe. But the lake was waiting for him, and the group activities were waiting for him, and, perhaps most terrible of all—

"Hope you like buffet-style dining!" Ricky chirped, holding open the door to Alexander's worst nightmare.

CHAPTER
ELEVEN

Theo was in a great mood. She actually loved buffet-style dining. A salad that was entirely mandarin oranges from a can? Yes! Only garlic bread and no spaghetti? Absolutely! Grainy chocolate milk and watery juice at the same time? You know it! Melty soft-serve ice cream during dinner instead of after? Bring it on! But they never went to buffets in their family out of respect for Alexander.

Alexander was in a miserable, hungry mood. He had eaten a banana and an orange. Both were already contained in a package, safely sealed away from bacteria and germs inside their peels.

They had been a little late to dinner, so most of the campers were already done. Theo still hadn't caught sight of Quincy. "Maybe they went to a different camp," she said, sitting on a log next to Alexander. The logs were positioned around a bonfire ring. Several of the counselors were feeding the bonfire, getting the flames higher and higher. It sent sparks into the black night sky, almost like adding stars to the darkness.

It was a lot easier to be happy about sitting in front of a bonfire with a full stomach than a mostly empty one. Alexander fidgeted, looking around for Wil and Edgar. But the brilliant golden orange of the flames made his eyes terrible in the dark, so everyone around them blurred together. They could all be Wil and Edgar and Quincy, for all he knew. Or they could be sitting right across from Edgaren't. He didn't feel safe and he didn't feel happy and he couldn't believe they'd be here for another week.

"I hope we have lake time first thing in the morning," Theo said. "I can't wait to do the rope swing."

Alexander said nothing. Theo knew he wasn't saying anything because he didn't feel the same way, but she held on to being excited. Was it wrong to want to have fun when they had a chance to? Hadn't they had enough weirdness and worry this summer? After all,

Wil herself had told them she wanted them to be happy and not stress out about things. What better place to do that than this very normal, very safe summer camp? She wished Alexander could see that. She'd have more fun if he was having fun.

She resolved to have fun anyway. Their mother's letter had told her to be brave and Alexander to be cautious, but it didn't seem like either of those applied here.

"I want to read that book." Alexander looked longingly over his shoulder to where their cabin and his book waited somewhere in the night. He hadn't had any time with it today. Camp Creek kept everyone busy all the time, and someone was always watching. "I think it could be important."

Theo resisted letting out an annoyed growl. "It's a book. It's not going anywhere."

"We both know that's not true when it comes to books. Not this summer. Important books have a way of being stolen."

"Who's to say that one's important? We have enough to worry about without you adding even more to the list." Theo took a deep breath, trying to be nicer. "Besides, Camp Creek is great."

"I don't like it here," Alexander whispered. He didn't

know whether the deep unease he felt was because something here was wrong, or because something was wrong with *him*. Either way, there was no chance he could relax and enjoy their time.

"S'mores!" Theo shouted, trying to change the subject.

Sure enough, sticks were passed around. Alexander noted the risk of gouging and impalement, with people walking around in the dark on uneven ground carrying long, sharpened sticks. Marshmallows were placed on the ends of those sticks. Alexander noted the risk of burns from molten marshmallow, to say nothing of everyone reaching into the same marshmallow bag with hands that were dubiously clean at best. Everyone began singing camp songs. Alexander noted the risk of being so horribly embarrassed by his voice cracking or not knowing the words that his heart might actually stop beating.

That didn't seem likely, but still. One never knew.

At last, the bonfire was over. Theo had eaten four s'mores. Alexander had eaten none. She nudged him with her shoulder as they followed Heidi and Ricky back toward their cabin. There were other children around them, but the night rendered them all anonymous.

"Your deconstructed s'mores are better," she said.

Alexander said nothing, because of course they were.

His deconstructed s'mores carried no risk of second-degree burns or impalement or bacterial contamination from grubby hands. And no one ever had to sing along to silly camp songs while eating them.

Their cabinmates rushed in ahead of them, then back out with their toothbrush kits. Alexander was mildly impressed that everyone here still cared about dental health. Cavities didn't take summer vacations after all. It took him and Theo longer to get their things out of their suitcases, so by the time they got to the bathrooms, their cabinmates were already gone, and by the time they were ready for bed, their cabinmates were all already tucked in beneath tie-dyed blankets. Everyone was wearing head-phones, which seemed a little odd.

"We'll get you yours tomorrow!" Heidi whispered, still with an exclamation mark. "They really help you get a good night's sleep!" As though to demonstrate, she put hers on, lay back, and was immediately out cold.

Only Theo and Alexander were still awake. Their bunks were against the wall closest to the door. It was dark in the cabin, the sound of lots of bodies breathing in unison oddly loud. Did everyone's breathing sync up like that when they were sleeping? Alexander couldn't re-member it happening in the bunk room at the Sanguine

Spa. There, he had weird dreams that ended up not being dreams at all, but rather Lucy, Mina's little sister, disrupting his sleep.

He wished she'd show up now. He wanted to be disrupted from this.

"Try to sleep, okay?" Theo whispered. She was pretty tired after such a long day, but so excited for tomorrow that it was going to be hard to sleep. She closed her eyes and practiced active meditation. Only instead of imagining a super-normal summer day, she imagined the best day ever for herself, full of zip lines and rope swings and canoeing. Part of her knew she should be on alert, be worried.

But then again, that's what she had Alexander for. Smiling to herself, she let her imagination run wild with what fun tomorrow would hold and plummeted into sleep like she was falling from a rope swing into a lake.

Alexander lay in the dark, alone, thinking about all the things that crept around at night in the woods. Thinking about his parents and where they might be. Thinking about how much easier it would be if he were like the other kids, all fast asleep after a full day of fun. Thinking, thinking, thinking, which was always his problem, wasn't it?

Alexander made a resolution. He would have a better day tomorrow. He would try not to think so much or worry so hard. Or, at the least, he would try to blend in well enough that they wouldn't design a whole game around him like Spot the Skulker. What would his be? Imitate the Introvert? Ring-Around-the-Worrier? No. His would be Spy the Crybaby.

Already feeling sick with humiliation over a game that didn't even exist, he turned onto his side and curled up. He wished he were home. He wished he had agreed to go back to Aunt Saffronia's house. He wished he were anywhere but here.

And then, just before he fell asleep, sad and homesick and miserable, he wished he were anyone but himself.

Maybe, at Camp Creek, he could pretend to be.

CHAPTER
TWELVE

Theo and Alexander woke up late. Somehow every other kid in the cabin had gotten up, gotten dressed, and was already out for the day before they even opened their eyes.

"Isn't it weird that no one wanted to sleep in?" Alexander asked. "Every kid here is an early riser?" That didn't seem likely. He wasn't prone to sleeping in, but even he didn't want to rise with the dawn during summer vacation.

Theo was frantically running fingers through her hair. She was trying to make it stick down but had rather the opposite effect. "Come on, we're going to be late!"

"For what?" Alexander asked. He sat on the edge of

his bed, slowly tying his shoelaces. He wanted nothing more than to stay in the cabin and read.

His stomach growled loudly, making him realize he wanted nothing more than to have a decent meal and *then* come back and read. He stroked the cover of his book longingly. It had been too dark in the cabin to read last night. But he couldn't skip breakfast, not after missing lunch and barely eating dinner.

"I need to read that book," he said.

"Right, yeah, sure. After breakfast. Come on!" Theo was bouncing with impatience. As soon as Alexander's shoelaces were tied—double-knotted so they wouldn't come undone and trip him—she grabbed his hand and dragged him down the road toward the cafeteria. They really were late. It was almost empty, with only Heidi and Ricky in there.

Alexander was disappointed. He still wanted to talk to Wil and Edgar. And Theo was disappointed, too, that there hadn't been a single cowgirl-hat sighting. But she wasn't too disappointed, because she had a rope swing in her near future.

"I made you breakfast!" Heidi declared, pointing to two bowls filled with multiple kinds of cereal.

"Oh, your specialty," Alexander said, trying to smile.

"Yes! You remembered!" Heidi was so genuinely delighted that Alexander sat and ate rather than risk hurting her feelings. As soon as the last spoonful was finished, Ricky waved for them to get up and follow him.

"Come on! We have to catch up! We're behind!"

Alexander walked as quickly as he could. He didn't want to ask what they were doing. But then he was imagining activities each more terrifying than the last—tree climbing, zip lining, rope swinging, or, worst of all, group skits—so he had to know what he was in for. "What's on the schedule?"

"Ceramics!" Heidi declared. "It's the best!"

"Just like everything else," Alexander said.

"Exactly!"

He smiled, relieved. He was okay at art. Surely he could handle ceramics. It was a nice way to ease into the rest of the day.

Theo was disappointed. She wanted to break the glassy surface of the lake with her plummeting body. But they were headed in the opposite direction, deeper into the trees.

"What's that building?" Theo pointed. A ways off the path was a small log cabin, every window covered with a tie-dyed curtain, even the smoke oozing up from the chimney was bright colors, like it didn't want to be left out by being drab gray.

"The tie-dye cabin!" Heidi said, but she didn't look at it, keeping her eyes firmly ahead. Ricky, too, didn't look over.

"Where you dye all the shirts?"

"I think so!" Heidi answered.

"It's hard to remember!" Ricky said.

"But so fun! And look, there's the ceramics building!" Heidi pointed. The building up ahead was built as a bridge over a bubbling creek. It was cool and green and shady in the woods, and all walls were made of screens so the room was open to the breeze and the noise of the creek. Even Alexander had to admit it was pretty great. There were lots of rails along the screens to prevent anyone from losing their balance and falling through into the water, but even if that happened, the creek was shallow and not dangerous.

A group of campers around their same age were sitting in a circle in the building, carefully shaping gray lumps of clay. They were bent over their work, focused and intent. They were also all in tie-dyed shirts, and everyone had a boondoggle-in-progress hooked to the belt loops on their shorts.

"You're doing great!" The camp counselor in charge of pottery blended in with every other counselor they had seen. Her hair was pulled back in a ponytail, and her face was a face that seemed made for smiling and nothing else. Her tie-dyed shirt was orange and yellow and red, and her khaki shorts were miraculously free from clay. "New campers! That's so exciting!" She gestured to two free spots.

"Go on!" Heidi said.

"You'll have so much fun!" Ricky beamed. "We'll see you later!"

The counselor with bright red hair and a pale white face and the counselor with a bright red face and pale white hair stood and waved at them until they were seated, then bounced back down the pathway.

"Hi!" the pottery counselor said. "I'm Georgie! We're making pinch pots! They're going to look like this when you're done!" She held up the example, a perfectly round, small pot with no obvious use or purpose.

"Can I make a dragon?" Theo asked.

"We're making pinch pots!" Georgie responded, beaming. "Your neighbor can help if you have any questions!"

Alexander was already hard at work on his pinch pot. This, at least, he knew he could do. Maybe they'd let him stay in the pottery class and make pinch pots all week. He liked it here, with the noise of water he didn't have to go in, and the breeze, and something simple to do that he knew he was capable of. And he liked this building, where he couldn't even see the lake or the games or anything else he was terrified of facing.

He could be good at this. He had to be.

Theo sighed, already feeling fidgety. She didn't want to make a silly pinch pot when there were other way more fun things to do. Bored, she turned to her neighbor. They hadn't officially met any of the kids in their cabin. This one was a pretty girl with black hair pulled back in a plain ponytail, wearing a tie-dyed shirt, khaki shorts, and tennis shoes. She smiled blandly as she made her pinch pot, her focus complete and total.

The girl looked so normal, so much like everyone else, that it took Theo several seconds to process who she was seeing. And even then she couldn't quite believe it. All this time—even last night—her target had been right there!

"Where's your *lasso*, Quincy?" Theo snapped.

CHAPTER
THIRTEEN

Quincy looked up at Theo and blinked with a glazed expression perfect for the ceramics building. "What lasso?" she asked, her smile blank and innocent.

"Those pots aren't going to pinch themselves!" Georgie chirped brightly in Theo's direction. "If they could do that, they wouldn't need us!"

Alexander squirmed, worried by proxy. He was diligently pinching his clay, but Theo was glaring at Quincy. At least, Alexander was pretty sure it was Quincy, though it didn't quite look like her and definitely didn't *seem* like her. So that was worry number one. If Quincy was here, did that mean her uncle

Edgaren't was, too? But worry number two was that Theo was going to get them in trouble, which would also get him in trouble, since they were a pair.

"Pinch while you interrogate," Alexander whispered, elbowing Theo.

She pinched her clay with more force than was necessary, squashing it over and over again. "Where's your uncle? Where's your hat? And where's your rope? If you think you're going to catch me off guard and tie me up like I tied you up, well, I'd like to see you try!"

Quincy was still smiling vaguely as she worked on her pot. "Rope? Do you mean my boondoggle?" She patted the elaborately braided plastic strips hooked onto her shorts by the belt loop.

"No, I don't mean your boondoggle! You can't lasso anyone with that."

Quincy laughed. "Why would I lasso someone?"

"Because it's what you do?"

"No, I do ceramics! And canoeing, and archery, and crafts, and—"

"Cut it out." Theo squished whatever progress she had made on her pot in a twitch of anger. This wasn't how she had imagined her confrontation with Quincy going. She hadn't figured out all the specifics, but it had involved a lasso-off that Theo would obviously win, followed by a tearful confession from her former friend. "Why are you acting like this?"

"Acting like what?" Quincy looked over, genuinely puzzled.

"Like we don't know you. Like we weren't just together at the spa, where you betrayed us."

"The spa?" Quincy frowned, but her smile popped back on as though it was a reflex. It was a very confusing facial expression on a very confused face. "Oh, the spa. I hadn't thought about that in ages. It was so long ago!"

"It was literally yesterday morning," Alexander said, then jumped as he realized he wasn't working on his pot. He hurriedly finished. Was it cheating to give his pot to Theo? Because she wasn't making any progress at all. But it wasn't like this was school, where they got assignments. No one was grading their pots, so it wasn't technically cheating to help someone else; they were here to have fun. Or at least, everyone *else* seemed to be having fun, smiling and humming a single note as they shaped their crafts.

Alexander waited until Georgie was looking in the other direction, then swapped his pot with Theo's abused clay. He was sweating and feeling guilty, but at least the counselor wouldn't get mad at Theo now. Alexander hurried to catch this clay up.

"Yesterday morning, when you betrayed us," Theo corrected him.

"That seems like a lifetime ago," Quincy said dreamily. "I remember it was a lot of work, and sometimes scary, and I felt weird and sad. Now I'm having the best summer. The summer every kid should have. I'm glad you both are, too!"

"Stop lying," Theo hissed. "Where's Edgaren't?"

Quincy laughed. "What kind of name is Edgaren't?"

"Heathcliff," Alexander corrected him. Edgaren't wasn't really his name, that was just what they called the man with the small, mean eyes and the large, mean mustache. Of course Quincy wouldn't call her own uncle that. "Or Van Helsing. Whatever his name is. Your uncle."

Quincy shrugged, putting the finishing touch on her pinch pot. "I don't know."

Theo gave Alexander a thunderously angry look. "She's lying to us about everything."

But Alexander wasn't so sure. Quincy seemed genuinely confused, like she could barely remember the spa.

"What if he did something to her?" Alexander asked. "To her memories or her brain?" He touched the side of his head, getting clay there and immediately wanting to wash it off. "I don't think she's faking."

"She didn't have a hard time faking being our friend." Theo smashed Alexander's loaned pinch pot flat. Alexander flinched, hurt and annoyed that he had worked hard on it *and* sort of cheated to give it to her, and Theo had smushed it. Couldn't she see he was trying hard to participate? To blend in?

With a huff, he went back to his second pinch pot, carefully smoothing the edges.

"Wow!" the counselor said, beaming at him. "You're a natural! That's the best pinch pot I've ever seen you make!"

Alexander sat up straighter, smiling.

"That's the *only* pinch pot she's ever seen you make," Theo grumbled, ruining it.

"And, Theo, that's a really great effort! I'm sure you'll get it!"

Theo flashed a fake smile and thumbs-up before digging her thumbs back into the clay, squashing whatever was left. She was in a terrible mood. Right when she had decided they'd have a fun day, she found what she was looking for. Sort of. Here was Quincy, but where were her answers? Quincy didn't even seem to feel guilty about what she had done, much less have an explanation that would make Theo feel less hurt.

And Theo didn't like feeling hurt. Feeling angry was easier.

"Okay! It's almost mandatory rest time!" The counselor gestured, and everyone stood in unison, smiling excitedly as they lined up to wash the drying clay off their hands. Theo stood behind Quincy, glaring at her back. While Alexander carefully cleaned anywhere he might have touched his face with his clay-covered hands, Theo grabbed several small metal tools and slipped them into her pocket.

As they followed the other campers back toward their cabin, Theo nudged a short, gap-toothed girl with a super-friendly smile. "Hey, do you know Quincy?"

"Sure! She's in our cabin! Go, Team Everything Good and Normal!"

"What has she told you about herself?"

"She likes sports, her favorite kind of cereal is anything with flakes, and if she were a color, she'd be sky blue!" The girl paused, smiling. "Actually, I made that last one up. But it feels right!"

"Have you seen her lasso?"

"Lasso?" The girl tilted her head. "What would she be doing with a lasso?"

"Everything. She can do everything with it." Theo had been jealous of what a great, weird skill it was. She had even learned some lassoing herself. It was bizarre seeing Quincy walking ahead of them with nothing in her hands, no spinning rope spelling out words in the air or snagging a water bottle from a table, or snatching betrayal out of friendship.

"She's really great at making boondoggles!" the girl offered.

"Has she told you about her family, or where she's from?" Alexander asked. He had also been hurt by Quincy, but he didn't take it personally, like Theo. Or rather, he took it personally in a different way. Theo took it as an attack of her trust. Alexander wondered what he might have been able to do to help Quincy, or to understand her better.

The gap-toothed friendly girl shook her head. "No, she didn't say anything about that."

Alexander stopped, shocked. "Wait. She didn't even tell you she's from Texas?"

The girl shrugged. "Nope!"

Alexander grabbed Theo's arm, making her stop as the rest of the cabin kept walking, oblivious.

"Theo. Something really *is* wrong with Quincy. There's no way someone from Texas wouldn't tell other people. It's like a requirement of being Texan. Don't you remember? That was the first thing she told us about herself. Come to think of it, she barely has her accent anymore. It's like someone took Quincy and made a copy of her, but the printer was running low on ink so everything is faded."

"Nothing here is faded," Theo grouched, gesturing to the campers. She had a point. They were all aggressively bright. But she also just wanted to argue. She was feeling stubborn and angry and frustrated. She wasn't about to trust that Quincy wasn't tricking them again. All her plans to enjoy the day were completely ruined.

Alexander was upset for a different reason. He suspected Quincy needed help, but he didn't know why or how. He couldn't see any threats. There was no sign of Edgaren't. And all the kids here seemed so happy, so friendly, so good at group situations. Maybe Quincy had been nervous at the spa, and they were seeing the real her now. Maybe Edgaren't really had just dropped her off for a great summer vacation.

That seemed highly unlikely. But Alexander couldn't find any other explanations. In a strange way, he was jealous of Quincy, walking in step with the other campers. Clearly, she had found a way to fit in. Maybe she came here for a fresh start, to leave all the stress from the spa behind her. Meanwhile Alexander and Theo had followed her here, dragging suspicion and trouble along like the world's worst luggage.

Alexander had a terrible thought. Were *they* the bad guys in this situation? Was that why he couldn't fit in here, or anywhere? He knew Edgaren't wasn't a good or nice person, but he still believed Quincy was. And here they were, following her, harassing her. Doubtless Theo was plotting something, judging by the way she glared at Quincy's back.

Theo was not, in fact, plotting. She was too angry and outraged to have any clear thoughts at all. Once they got to the cabin, she opened her mouth to demand answers from Quincy. But all the other campers immediately went to their bunks and lay down on top of their covers.

"What's going on?" Theo asked. She noted which bunk Quincy was in, but didn't see any signs of a cowboy hat or a hidden rope. She'd search for them later.

"It's almost time for our mandatory rest," half the kids answered at once. They all closed their eyes.

"Hi!" Counselor Heidi said, appearing behind them. "Alexander and Theo, wow, it's so exciting to have you here for your first full day! You're supposed to go to the tie-dye cabin during mandatory rest time! I'm sorry you're going to miss resting, but you'll get to join us tomorrow! Tie-dye is exactly what you need to blend in! You'll love it! Remember to go in one at a time!"

"Why?" Alexander asked. He usually wanted Theo with him to help him feel braver. But he was still a little annoyed at her for her behavior in the ceramics session, when he had been trying hard and she hadn't even noticed. Maybe he didn't want to tie-dye with her, after all.

"The room isn't big enough for two!" Heidi climbed into an empty bunk and closed her eyes. Then, from speakers that Theo and Alexander couldn't see, that same layered tone that had blared yesterday after active meditation played.

It was obnoxious. Theo and Alexander didn't understand how anyone could rest through it. But all their cabinmates were lying peacefully, eyes closed, small smiles on their faces. Theo couldn't think straight with that noise happening.

"What do we do now?" Theo asked, grabbing Alexander's hand and pulling him out of the cabin.

"Where's Wil?" Alexander peered around. Wil had said she'd take them to tie-dye.

"I don't know. Maybe she's mandatorily resting." Theo folded her arms, wishing she had another clay pot to squash. Not only had she not done anything exciting so far today, she had finally found Quincy, but all she had discovered was that Quincy was still a lying liar who lied.

"We're supposed to go to tie-dye." Alexander shifted his weight from foot to foot. He didn't want to break rules, or mess up the schedule, or get in trouble. Especially not on their first full day, when they had to stay here a whole week now. The idea of making Heidi or Ricky sad or mad was terrible.

"Wil said she'd take us."

"But Wil isn't here, and Heidi told us to go. We know where it is." Alexander was annoyed with Wil. She had said they'd find answers, and now she was a camp counselor. She had said she'd take them to tie-dye, and now it was time and she wasn't here.

"Well, come on. Quincy reminded me that we're here for a reason. We can snoop. Maybe we'll find something Wil didn't." Theo slammed the cabin door closed, but none of the campers even flinched or startled at the sound.

Alexander didn't mind the idea of doing tie-dye. Heidi had promised it was what they needed to blend in. His mom always insisted that being your own self was better than being a self other people wanted you to be, but in this camp where everyone seemed to fit in, he really did want to be more like them.

Besides which, he had a feeling this was going to be one of the only other activities he was good at. Unless it was messy. Oh *no*, it was definitely going to be messy. But maybe he'd be so good at it, they'd let him be the camp tie-dyer, and he could avoid all the other activities that scared him.

"Yeah," he agreed. "We'll snoop." But, for once, Alexander lied. He really did just want to tie-dye, to swirl himself in bright colors and hope that, somehow, it made him feel less afraid.

CHAPTER
FOURTEEN

Alexander and Theo made their way down the tree-lined trail to the tie-dye cabin. It was weird that none of the counselors accompanied them, since everything else in camp seemed to involve oversight. Being watched by someone in charge made Alexander feel comforted, and Theo feel persecuted.

"Where do you think Wil is?" Alexander asked, mildly worried.

"Probably staring at her hand in despair, missing Rodrigo."

"It's weird that she and Edgar are counselors now, right? And how did she know that clapping game? And why was she participating? Wil isn't a participator." It

109

was one of the biggest things she and Alexander had in common.

"I don't know." Theo kicked a rock, watching it skitter away. "Why is Quincy pretending like she can't remember what happened at the spa, and that she doesn't like lassoing things?"

"Do you wish—" Alexander stopped, staring at the tie-dyed curtains obscuring the building ahead of them.

"That I could eat peanut butter with my fingers without having to wash them after?"

Alexander rolled his eyes. "No, do you wish—"

"That I could selectively turn off gravity and line all the walls and floor and ceiling with pillows so I could bounce around like a pinball?"

Alexander gave Theo a gentle push. His voice was soft. "Do you wish this was a normal camp and we were here for a normal time and could enjoy it without worrying about when Edgaren't will show up, and what he's up to, and where our parents are, and why Aunt Saffronia couldn't come with us, and why Wil is acting weird, or at least a different weird than her usual weird, and whether or not we can find those stolen books, and what's in them, and why . . ." Alexander trailed off, gesturing vaguely. "Why this whole summer, I guess?"

"Do *you* wish that?" Theo was surprised. She had wished exactly that and decided to act as though her wish had already come true, clear up until she found Quincy. But she couldn't believe Alexander felt that way. Camp Creek had so many forced group activities, many involving lake water and buffet-style eating. All those things were among Alexander's worst nightmares, right up there with toilet alligators.

But she didn't want to bring those up and add to his list of worries, since who knew what the sewer pipes connected to way out here.

"Yeah. I kind of do." Alexander sighed, reaching out and touching one of the huge swaths of tie-dyed material hanging on the cabin exterior. "It would be easier if we were here as campers, you know?"

"But even if Edgaren't weren't possibly lurking, and we didn't have all these mysteries and stuff, you wouldn't like this camp."

"I know." Alexander looked down at his double-knotted shoelaces, shoving his hands in his pockets. "I wish I could like it, too."

It bothered Theo, how sad Alexander seemed. He had been mad at her at the spa after she sort of accidentally lied to him so he'd break the rules, and he had been defiant at the water park when she bullied him into going down the slide without a raft. Both of those things she could react to. Push back against. But Alexander *sad?* She didn't know how to fix it, and when she didn't know how to fix things or how to fight them, she got flustered and uncomfortable.

The bees were beginning to buzz around her chest, working themselves up into a frenzy. Their parents knew how to help Alexander when he was like this. How to comfort him, reassure him. But their parents weren't here, and it was all so frustrating and aggravating that it made Theo want to be reckless. She was tired of being reckful.

But she'd take care of her brother, in the only way she could think to. "I'll go in first so I can tell you what to expect," she said. It was the kindest thing she could offer Alexander right now. He hated going into new situations. He never went first—not when they were born, tugged into the world by Theo's grip on his hand, and not once since. Theo blazed their way, and Alexander followed carefully behind.

Alexander moved aside the cloth in front of the door. "Here, hold on to this for me, just in case I have to change into those silly shorts." He passed her his magnifying glass. "I'm going first."

Theo watched in shock as Alexander walked inside without her.

She barely got a glimpse inside of what was, unsurprisingly, a room covered in tie-dye colors before the door swung shut again, sealing her away from Alexander. At least he would be safe in there, Theo thought to herself. After all, it was only tie-dyeing. The worst thing that could happen was he'd make a mess and be upset about it.

Theo was very, very wrong about that.

CHAPTER
FIFTEEN

Theo decided to start her snooping with the office. If campers weren't allowed there, then it was exactly where she wanted to go. Maybe there would be check-in information for Quincy, and she could find out details about Edgaren't. His real name, his phone number and address, his exact evil plans. Who knew what people put on those forms? She didn't. She'd never filled one out or even bothered to read them. Or sign them properly, a fact that had saved them at Fathoms of Fun.

Theo avoided the path, choosing to walk through the trees instead, in case she ran into any counselors who might ask where she was going or why she wasn't with a group. But she needn't have bothered. Apparently, afternoon rest time was mandatory for everyone. She didn't see a soul out. But she could still hear that terrible tone broadcasting.

Maybe she would break into the office and find the books Edgaren't had stolen. Or, better, find the books and also a note that her parents were on their way to pick them up right now. Or, best, find the books and also a note that her parents were on their way and also a tearful apology from Quincy that Theo could firmly reject and then feel better about everything.

Theo would have solved it all in five minutes and still have plenty of time to do the rope swing into the lake before her parents got here.

Then again, she knew even rejecting a tearful apology wouldn't solve the hurt that Quincy caused. And it wouldn't solve the hurt that their parents disappearing like that had left behind, or the damage the fear and worry had done. Not only to her, but to Alexander, especially. She was so mad at their parents for making Alexander even more worried and afraid than he normally was.

Maybe there was a good reason they were gone. A part of Theo even hoped they were actually missing. That gave her a goal, something to do, something to fight against. And it hurt less, the idea that they hadn't *wanted* to leave for the summer, but they'd been forced to.

Then again, maybe she'd get into the office and find Edgaren't and Quincy laughing at her and how silly she was and how much they'd liked tricking her. Theo's fists clenched. She would get into that office no matter what.

Avoiding the front reception entrance where Kiki was probably keeping a cheerful watch, Theo stayed outside and worked her way to the back of the office building. There were a few small windows there. Theo went up on her tiptoes and pressed her face against the glass. But they were curtained, so all she saw was a multicolored haze. Maybe she could get one of the windows open. She'd need a distraction, though, to draw everyone out of the office first. It wouldn't make any sense to crawl through a window and land in Dr. Jay's lap. The bland woman seemed pleasant enough, but it was more explaining than Theo cared to do.

She couldn't settle on an ideal diversion, though. Fire seemed excessive and dangerous. She'd need a co-conspirator to pull the whole "oh no, my friend is injured!" charade, but with Alexander busy and Quincy her enemy, she was out of coconspirators. And she hadn't seen any catchable wild animals like raccoons or toilet alligators that she could set loose in the reception area of the office.

Just when she was about to try the standard scream-bloody-murder-then-be-gone-before-they-get-here tactic, a hand reached out from under the building. It grabbed her ankle with a viselike grip, which made screaming bloody murder almost happen anyway. But Theo had been through a lot the last couple of weeks, so she held it in.

"You'd better let go of me if you know what's good for you." Theo's heart pounded as she looked straight down at the pale hand extending from a crawl space beneath the office building, clutching her ankle so tightly it was almost painful. But it wasn't a large hand, like Edgaren't had. It was a kid's hand, like her own.

"You'd better hide if you know what's good for you," a voice whispered harshly. The hand snaked back into the darkness.

Theo had wanted to break into the office for answers, but maybe she needed to break *under* the office instead. She got down onto her belly and scooted into the crawl space. It was dim and smelled like dirt. Unlike Alexander, she didn't once think about what kind of creatures would live under a building. She only had eyes for the creature hiding there. Up ahead of her, a pair of shoes were scooting away.

"Wait!" Theo hissed.

The shoes paused. Theo army-crawled. A face turned toward her, pale like a grub and streaked with dirt. He might have been wearing a tie-dyed shirt, but it was impossible to tell with how filthy he was.

"Who are you?" Theo asked. "Henry?"

"Henry. Hide," he said.

"I don't need to hide."

"You should follow my advice. Otherwise they'll change you."

"Who will change me?"

Henry pointed upward.

"The camp?"

He nodded, eyes glowing with an almost-feral light. Theo half considered setting *him* loose in reception. Surely he was about the same as a raccoon or a toilet alligator.

"Don't let them change you," he urged.

Theo scoffed. "Nothing can change me. I'm exactly how I should be." A lot of people had tried to change her. She had one teacher a few years ago who had insisted everything she did was wrong. It had hurt her feelings and her confidence a lot. But her parents had always been there to fight for her, to help her figure out how she learned best, eventually getting her put in a different class with a teacher who appreciated Theo's strengths.

Theo wasn't perfect—she knew she wasn't—but she liked herself. She was coordinated and strong and funny and loyal and very, very brave, and no silly summer camp could change any of that. If anything, she was perfectly suited to this camp already.

Henry glowered at her. "You're not how they think you should be."

"I don't care what they think. Who are *they*, anyway?"

He pointed upward again. She assumed he meant whoever was in the office and not the actual floorboards themselves. Then again, he was a boy living in a hole underneath a building, so maybe he really did think the floorboards were secretly trying to change them all and this was his way of avoiding them.

"Listen," Theo said, not sure Henry was the type of person with answers but willing to try anyway, "have you seen a man with small, mean eyes and a large, mean mustache?"

Henry shook his head. "I don't go out when anyone can see me, so I never see anyone."

"Right. Okay. Have you seen a bunch of books, then? Fancy books with locks, probably in a big trunk."

"Why should I tell you?" he snapped.

"Because it's important."

"To you, maybe. Not to me."

"Listen, have you seen them or—"

The floorboards creaked overhead, sending down a sprinkling of dust like the powdered sugar on a perfect doughnut, only without the doughnut, and the powdered sugar was gross dirt that made Theo's nose wrinkle up to hold in a sneeze.

"Stay out of my hiding spots!" Henry hissed. He crawled away into the darkness.

"Wait!" Theo closed her eyes and sneezed. When she opened her eyes, she couldn't see Henry anymore. She crawled after him but hit a dead end of cement. A search of the entire space beneath the office building revealed nothing. Henry had disappeared.

CHAPTER

SIXTEEN

By the time Theo wriggled free from the crawl space beneath the office, she was filthy. She couldn't go back to the tie-dye cabin like this. She'd have to explain why she looked like she'd been practicing burrowing like a small animal, when clearly it wasn't on the schedule.

Or maybe it was; she hadn't actually looked at the schedule. For all she knew, Henry was participating in a proud Camp Creek tradition of spending part of the day as a mole person.

Either way, she needed new clothes. She hurried past the office and down the pathway that led along the lakeshore to her cabin. It looked like mandatory rest time was over, and at some point—probably when she had been beneath the office—the stupid bell thing had stopped playing.

As Theo walked, she watched the lake activities, more than a little jealous of all the kids enjoying themselves instead of having to solve mysteries. One of the campers grabbed hold of the rope, whooped with joy, and swung out wide over the lake.

Which shouldn't have been remarkable—she'd watched many campers do the same—but it wasn't so much the rope swinging as the rope swinger that was shocking.

Alexander had just done the rope swing.

Alexander.

Alexander.

Theo stood, staring, her mouth open in surprise. Alexander surfaced, spitting water, and he didn't look panicked or worried or scared at all. He was . . . smiling.

What was going on? Alexander would never willingly go off a rope swing. There weren't enough safety features. He wouldn't even go on most of the slides at Fathoms of Fun, even though they had all been safety tested. (She assumed. Actually, she had no idea.)

Going off a rope swing into a lake? Theo had been

in enough of these types of situations with Alexander to know just a fraction of the things he would be worried about. Rope burn, forgetting to let go, letting go at the wrong time, belly flopping, the kid after him going too soon and crashing into him, not to mention lake bacteria or amoebas or brain-eating algae. He'd be able to tell her about some family in some place in some lake that went swimming and the water went up their noses and their brains boiled.

(She wasn't sure of the specifics, because things like that didn't stick in her head the same way they did in Alexander's. He remembered every bad thing that had ever happened to anyone that he had heard about.)

When Alexander emerged from the lake, not at all upset about how many microbes and bacteria and brain-eating amoeba he might have let in through his nose and mouth, he grabbed a tie-dyed shirt. That was another weird thing. Not only was he not wearing swim goggles—he refused to put his head underwater without swim goggles—but also Alexander never swam without a shirt. He was too worried about sunburns and skin cancer. He used the shirt to wipe off his face before dropping it on the ground instead of folding it and setting it carefully on a rock so it wouldn't get dirty.

Several of the campers patted him on the shoulder, and he laughed and patted them back, a perfectly normal casual interaction that, for Alexander, was anything but normal.

"Alexander!" Theo shouted. He looked up at her and waved brightly before *getting in line for the rope swing again*. Even when Alexander liked something mildly exciting, he always had to take a break to calm down and reset before he wanted to do it again.

Was this how he was snooping? Trying to blend in, lull Quincy into complacency so he could get answers? It was a brilliant idea, but Theo didn't understand how Alexander was managing it. He was acting like a complete stranger.

Theo rushed over. "What are you doing?" she yelled up the ladder, where Alexander was halfway to the top.

"Going on the rope swing!" he answered.

"Why?"

"Because everyone else is!" He gave her a thumbs-up, and she couldn't believe he was only holding on to a ladder with one hand, instead of strangling it in a death grip. "Hey, you're late for your tie-dye session!"

Alexander was right. Theo was due at the tie-dye cabin, and if she didn't show up on time, the counselors would start paying more attention to her. Then how was she supposed to successfully snoop? Was Alexander trying to warn her that they were on to her? Is that why he was doing this?

"Be careful," she cautioned.

Alexander laughed. "I don't need to be careful. We're just having fun!"

What was happening here? Who was this stranger in place of her brother? Frustrated and confused, Theo ran to their cabin. Their suitcases were unpacked. She didn't like the idea of someone going through her stuff. She rummaged in the drawers next to her bed and found a clean shirt and pair of shorts to change into, throwing her dirty clothes on top of the bed. They landed on something unexpected. She pushed them aside to find a pair of odd sunglasses with purple lenses. They reminded her of the ones the fake Mrs. Widow had worn to hide the fact that she had the real Mrs. Widow locked away in a tower.

Were they the same pair? Where had they come from? How long had they been there? She hadn't checked her bed when they came in for mandatory rest time, too busy watching Quincy instead.

Wear them so you can still see, a note scrawled on a scrap of rainbow paper said.

"What's going on here?" Theo didn't know what the purpose of the glasses was. Maybe they were from one of the counselors. Or maybe they were from Wil and Edgar. But Wil would know that Theo had perfect vision and didn't need glasses to be able to see. So why leave them for her?

Besides which, the last person she had seen with the fake Mrs. Widow was Edgaren't. So maybe they were from him, and they were a trick. Theo had way too many questions and no one to ask them to. She shoved the glasses under her pillow and went back outside.

Alexander had emerged from the water again. He put his shirt on—his new tie-dyed one, a bright and garish clash of colors that anywhere else would make him the center of attention, but at Camp Creek made him one of the crowd.

"Alexander," Theo said, grabbing his arm and pulling him away from the group heading toward the volleyball net. "I have to tell you what happened. And you can tell me about the tie-dye."

"Isn't it great?" He gestured at his shirt. It looked like an entire vat of children's lollipops had vomited all over it.

"Yeah, but what happened in the tie-dye cabin? Who helped you? Was Wil there?"

Alexander's smile faded a bit, and his eyebrows drew closer together. "I can't— It was—I— Well, I dyed my shirt. Isn't it great?"

"Yeah," Theo repeated, alarm bells going off in her head, all her bees swarming. "Listen, now that we know Quincy *is* here, I think we should break into the office."

Alexander laughed. "Why would we do that?"

"To find answers! Clues!"

"But it's beach sports on the schedule right now, and my team needs me." He pointed to where several other kids, including Quincy, were gesturing for him to join them in a volleyball game.

"You want to play?"

"Of course I do! Everyone else is." Alexander smiled. Then he ran to join the others. They threw him the ball, and he didn't flinch, or claim he had a stomachache, or sneak off to read instead of playing. He joined right in, like he'd been playing group sports his whole life.

Something was very, very wrong.

A hand came down on Theo's shoulder. She turned to find herself looking at a beaming Wil and a grinning Edgar.

"There you are!" Wil said. "I'm so glad you went to your cabin to change!"

"We've been looking for you!" Edgar gestured toward the path. "It's time for your tie-dye session!"

"She's dye-ing to meet you!" Wil said, then laughed. Edgar laughed, too. And three counselors walking by laughed as well, because Wil and Edgar were laughing, so they joined in. Wil and Edgar high-fived them on the way and led Theo down the path toward the cabin where her brother had gone in as Alexander and come out as a stranger.

And now it was Theo's turn.

CHAPTER
SEVENTEEN

Theo watched Wil and Edgar ahead of her. They spoke only in exclamation marks. They bounced while they walked, even their steps super excited to be doing whatever they were doing. And they were both wearing tie-dye, just like Alexander.

They had probably gone into that cabin, too, and come out like—well, like whoever they were now. Something was wrong, and it started with the tie-dye.

Theo should have been scared. But she wasn't good at being scared. She was good at moving, and spatial awareness, and climbing, and geometry, and fixing things, and being angry when she should be other things.

Theo threw back her shoulders and marched straight

to the cabin door. "Bring it on," she said, glaring at the tie-dye draped there.

Wil patted her shoulder. "Protect your eyes! Safety first!" she said, then opened the door for Theo to go inside.

Theo stepped in, some of her bravery overwhelmed by the sheer visual confusion. She didn't know where to look, or what she was looking at, or even how the room was shaped or what type of room it was. It felt like she had entered another dimension, a dimension filled with swirling colors and clashing patterns, a tie-dyed mess of cheerful chaos.

It was an assault on the eyes, so much so that Theo didn't see the woman in the center of the room, draped head to toe in tie-dye, until she moved.

Theo yelped, raising both her hands karate-style.

"Hello." Dr. Jay's voice was smooth and calm. Her face, in contrast to what she wore, remained remarkably bland. In the time since she had first met Dr. Jay yesterday, Theo had already forgotten what she looked like. If Theo had had to describe Dr. Jay to a sketch artist, all she could have said was *Imagine the most normal-looking woman you've ever seen. Now make her even more normal, so normal you forget her face as soon as you look away. Draw that.*

"I didn't see you there," Theo said, scowling to cover her embarrassment over being startled.

"Didn't you?" Dr. Jay asked, looking down at her clipboard. "Ah, yes. Theodora Sinister-Winterbottom. What a name to be burdened with!"

"I like my name." Theo did not, in fact, like her name, and she did, in fact, think it was ridiculous and too long. But no one else got to say that. "I go by Theo, though."

"I see. How do you like Camp Creek so far?"

"It's complicated." Theo folded her arms.

"Well, that's concerning. It should be simple." Dr. Jay didn't talk in all exclamation marks like the camp counselors, which was both a relief—it was a lot of emotion to be constantly subjected to—and a bit jarring. Hearing a calm, melodic voice in the middle of all this visual chaos didn't make sense. It made Theo feel like she was about to lose her balance. "You're a child. You're at summer camp. It should be a break."

"A break from what?" Theo demanded. She looked anxiously around the room. Were there other people hidden? Was Edgaren't in tie-dyed camouflage, waiting to grab her? What had happened in here that had changed Alexander, Wil, and Edgar?

"A summer break! A real one. Sunshine and laughter,

friends, games, swimming, nothing to worry about, nothing to be afraid of."

"I'm not afraid of anything," Theo insisted. And even though Theo was very brave, she knew it was a lie. Because she was afraid of something. Several somethings now. The way Alexander was acting made her afraid. The way her parents were gone made her afraid. And how much she actually did want a summer with nothing to worry about, how that idea created a sort of ache inside her like a hook, dragging her away from what was *important* toward what was *easy*, made her afraid.

Because it would be really easy to have fun here. To run out and join Alexander. To not question why Alexander was being so weird, but enjoy having a twin who wanted to do the same things as her for once. To stop worrying about whether or not Edgaren't was lurking, or where the books were, or what Wil wasn't telling them, or what Quincy was up to.

Theo was afraid that, if she wasn't careful and determined, if she didn't listen to her bees telling her things in this room were extremely strange and alarmingly off, she might give up and listen to this woman's promise of a normal summer.

It was hard, being different. And it was hard, being brave.

Maybe, without Alexander here being afraid to make her extra brave to protect him, Theo wasn't brave at all.

But just because Alexander didn't seem to be afraid anymore didn't mean she wouldn't look out for him. And looking out for him meant not giving up, or letting her guard down, or allowing this Dr. Jay to tell her what type of summer she should be having.

"Sit, sit." Dr. Jay pointed to a stool that Theo hadn't seen because it was draped in blue-and-pink cloth. Theo sat while Dr. Jay moved a covered table in front of her. In the center of the table was a bin for catching die. Dr. Jay put a flat wire frame on top of it, and on top of that she placed a pristinely white shirt. It was all Theo could focus her poor eyeballs on, a single point of calm in the middle of the swirling vortex of this room.

"Is that dirt in your hair?" Dr. Jay asked, her tone suddenly sharper, less melodic and soothing.

Theo reached up. Sure enough, there was dirt in her hair. Probably from the dust that had rained down on her while she was under the office building with Henry.

"Did you find him? My nephew?" Dr. Jay came around

the table and bent over, studying Theo's face, looking for a lie. "It's important that he sees me. He needs help. He might not think so, but I know what's best, and I won't let any children escape."

"Escape?" Theo asked, alarmed.

"I mean be lost. I won't let any children be lost. I worry about him, running around feral out there. Well. If you see him, you'll tell me." She said it as though it were fact. As though Theo had no choice in the matter. She pulled several bottles of dye out of her pockets and set them down in front of Theo. "I'll leave you to it. Listen to the music, let everything wash over you, let your mind soak up the colors just like that shirt."

Dr. Jay swished out between two curtain panels. Music began playing, but it wasn't really music. It was that single note, the one that had played earlier during mandatory resting time.

And then, impossibly, the entire room *began to spin*. Slowly at first, so Theo doubted it was happening. But then faster, the walls spinning around her, the shirt in front of her the only point of stillness to keep her eyes on so she wouldn't feel too dizzy.

The whole thing was entrancing. That music tone, the swirling, spinning colors, her eyes fixed on the white while everything else moved in the background. She saw the colors without seeing them, absorbed them without meaning to. She picked up one of the bottles of dye and held it over the shirt. Her eyes began to water, everything blurring.

This was the best thing to do. She wanted to do this. She wanted a shirt like everyone else's. She wanted to be part of Camp Creek. She wanted the summer every child should have.

Theo leaned forward, and her pocket clunked against the table. Alexander's magnifying glass! She pulled it out, desperate for something else to focus her eyes on. Then she held it up, closing one eye and peering through it with the other.

Just like that, the room came into focus. The angle of the magnifying lens slowed the spinning, magnified the colors, and broke up the patterns. It revealed everything in a new way.

Now Theo could see that the swirls of color on the walls weren't random. There were words hidden in them, spinning all around her. Her eyes must have been reading them even when her brain couldn't keep up. She saw the word HAPPY, the word CALM, the word OBEDIENT. And, over and over again, the word NORMAL.

Her eyeballs were relieved, at last, to be able to understand what they were seeing. But that terrible, incessant noise! Already she was humming along to it, trying to match the notes. She pulled out her antique timer and wound it, holding it against her ear so she could hear the steady, reliable *tick-tick-tick* of it.

Much like the magnifying glass, it helped her separate and make sense of the noise she was hearing. Because the tone wasn't just one tone. Now that she was able to really listen, to break it into smaller pieces by giving it a beat, she heard several notes played at once. Under the notes was a single voice: Dr. Jay, droning "Normal, normal, normal" over and over again.

"What the *what*," Theo whispered to herself. What would have happened if Theo hadn't used Alexander's magnifying glass and her stopwatch? Would she have absorbed these sights and sounds without meaning to? Some sort of subliminal messaging to reprogram her brain, soaking in like the dye for the shirt she was supposed to be coloring?

Theo glanced around. There was no way to tell whether or not she was being watched. So she pasted a smile on her face. She wasn't sure what Dr. Jay expected to be happening now—if the kids normally fainted, or started babbling, or stood on their heads and recited the alphabet backward, but those all seemed too weird. Dr. Jay wanted normal. Theo figured she'd pretend like she was having a good time.

She squeezed the first bottle of dye on her shirt. And then the next. And then the next, and the next, and the next, until every bottle was empty and the entire shirt and bin beneath it was one big slopping mess of dye.

The room slowly stopped spinning, and the music turned off. Theo shoved the magnifying glass back in her pocket and tucked her timer under her shirt right as Dr. Jay swept in, a smile like a sprinkle of cinnamon on her bland oatmeal face. But the smile froze there, then was absorbed into the oatmeal, disappearing.

"Oh," she said as Theo held up her work. Her fingers were stained so many dark colors they looked like they were rotting off. Theo's shirt wasn't a bright burst of color. All the dyes had mixed together to create a solid black mess.

"Well," Dr. Jay said, gingerly taking the shirt between her fingers. "I'll just . . . get this rinsed and dried for you. Sometimes it takes a few sessions for things to soak in. You'll come back tomorrow."

"Can't wait!" Theo chirped, beaming. She walked out

as though she didn't have a care in the world, but as soon as she was free, she collapsed against the wall of the cabin. It was dark out, the stars winking to life above her. How long had she been in there?

Theo put a hand against her racing heart. She had done it. She was still herself. But she now had a terrifying theory:

Whatever that combination of music and dye and spinning and words was, it was brainwashing the campers with subliminal messages. Forcing them to be happy, to be obedient, to fit in. To be normal.

However Dr. Jay was doing it, Theo couldn't deny that it worked. That cabin was changing kids. It had already changed her brother and sister.

And Theo had no idea how to fix it.

CHAPTER

EIGHTEEN

Theo gave herself a few moments to lean against the wall and think about that swirling room. About how Alexander had gone in himself and had come out someone else.

She wasn't afraid anymore. She was mad. Really, really mad. She loved Alexander. Sure, sometimes he was frustrating, and sometimes she wondered how they were twins when they were so different. But he was *her* Alexander, and no one else got to decide to change him.

Theo stomped down the path, wishing her bees were real and she could send them ahead of herself like a buzzing, swarming army, ready to deliver stinging revenge. She meant to march straight to the cabin and find Alexander, but something caught her eye.

The office lights were all off. No one was inside. And, even better, one of the tie-dyed curtains was stirring gently in the breeze. Which meant that window was open.

She needed to get to Alexander, but this might be her best shot at the office. Wondering if Henry was creeping around somewhere beneath her, she grabbed the window ledge and hauled herself up. The window was an easy squeeze, and Theo slid down into the interior office without a sound.

It was dim, but her eyes had adjusted to the darkness outside. It looked like a regular old boring office. There was a frosted glass doorway leading out into the hall to the reception area, and a door to what was probably a closet next to a bookshelf with several books, none of which looked fun. There were a couple of chairs facing a desk. On the desk was a bulky telephone, but no computer. Which was just as well. Theo wasn't like Wil. She could use computers when she needed to, but they were boring and she had no idea how to do anything fancy or sneaky on them.

The desk had several drawers. Theo moved the desk

chair aside and tugged on the top drawer. Locked. Then the next, and the next. All locked. One locked drawer she could understand. But *all* of them locked? They were definitely hiding something.

Theo crouched, pulling out the tools she'd aggressively borrowed from the ceramics building. She assumed she'd be a natural at lockpicking.

She assumed wrong. Five minutes later, she was still fiddling around, poking the interior of the lock hoping something happened. She wanted to scream, to throw the tools, to knock the desk over.

Instead, she closed her eyes and took some deep breaths. Remembered her father tinkering on his battle bots. He'd spend hours doing the same basic task over and over, trying to figure out the best way to wire something. Or her mother, baking batch after batch of cookies with the tiniest of changes in ingredients, baking time, or temperature, all in search of the perfect combination.

And if Alexander were here, he'd advise her to be cautious, to take her time.

Theo could do this. She slowed down and paid attention to how the interior of the lock felt depending on how she moved her tools. She eased one direction and then the next, like exploring a tiny, invisible cave. And then, to her surprise, something clicked. The drawer popped open.

Whatever Theo had been expecting inside, it hadn't been this. She was looking at Alexander's book about camps. When had they taken it? And why would they lock it up? Unless there was important information inside. Theo wanted to take the book with her back to their cabin, but she had nowhere to hide it. Plus, if she took it now, the camp director would know someone had been in the office and could get past the locks.

She flipped the cover open and gasped. Their mother's letter was inside, also stolen and locked away. It made Theo furious to see it here, when it belonged with them. Obviously Dr. Jay didn't want anyone reading this book. Which meant Theo had to. It was a risk, though. If they found out she took it . . .

But what if they didn't find out? If it was locked in a drawer, odds were no one was using it very often. She scurried to the bookshelf, running her fingers along the spines. They were all slightly dusty. No one was reading these books. And there! A book the same size as Alexander's camp book, also hardcover with a removable dust jacket. She pulled it out, adjusting the books to cover up the hole. The book was called *Adventures in Advertising,* which didn't seem adventurous at all.

Theo carefully removed the dust jackets of both books. Then she swapped them. Now it looked like *A History of Summer Camps and the Unexplained Disappearances of Various Campers in the Mountainous Lake Regions* was *Adventures in Advertising,* but, more importantly, it looked like *A History of Summer Camps and the Unexplained Disappearances of Various Campers in the Mountainous Lake Regions* was still locked away in this drawer, in case anyone checked on it.

But the letter. She had no way of faking a replacement for that. There were no envelopes or sheets of paper that she could see, and she'd never been able to imitate her mother's handwriting. It had to stay here for now.

Reluctantly, Theo closed the drawer and locked it again. The next locked drawer took half the time to pick and revealed several lengths of familiar rope. Quincy's ropes. Theo slammed that drawer shut, not wanting to think about what it meant that Quincy's beloved lassos were locked up. The rest of the drawers contained things that obviously meant something to a kid but were now locked away.

Theo didn't dare take anything else, but she noted it all. Then she tiptoed over to the closet door. It, too, was locked. The floorboards creaked beneath her feet, and she remembered the shower of dust as she crawled under them.

Which made her think of exploring that space. She carefully paced the length of the room. If she was right, the cement she had run into beneath the building was exactly at this closet. Why did only the closet have a cement foundation, while the rest of the building was supported by beams?

Curious.

There was a noise from the reception area. Theo was out of time. She grabbed the book and shoved it under her shirt, then slipped out the window. Once she was through, she closed the window almost all the way, so it would look shut but not be latched. Hopefully no one would notice.

Then she hurried around the side of the building, coming out next to the lodge. The bonfire was burning on the shore, the light reflecting like points of flame out on the lake. Theo marched straight up to it but paused before she was illuminated. Alexander was across from her, revealed in the orange flicker. He was sitting next to

Quincy. They both smiled, holding marshmallows on long sticks over the fire.

Alexander didn't look like he was worried about the potential fire hazards. She didn't see him warn anyone about the temperature of a burning marshmallow, and how badly it would hurt if molten mallow got flung onto someone's skin. And he didn't cringe as the bag was passed around and kid after kid stuck their hand in, contaminating the whole bag with whatever germs they had on their grubby lake-water camp fingers.

He was enjoying roasting a marshmallow, doing camp things with other happy campers. Theo stayed where she was, wondering: Did the cabin change Alexander, or did Alexander *want* to change? Hadn't he said he wished he could fit in? Could do camp things without being scared or worrying over every part of them?

Because Theo was still standing in the darkness, no one noticed her. Which was how she heard two adults talking from the direction of the office. One was clearly Dr. Jay. And the other was too quiet for Theo to overhear.

"It doesn't always work," Dr. Jay said, sounding frustrated, nothing soothing about her voice now. "There are the unusually difficult cases, the ones who refuse to accept suggestions made for their own benefit. Like my wretched nephew. But we can't have that here. We owe her this. This time, I'll fix these kids. I'll do it right, because no one was there to do it right for us. And, if I can't, we'll send them to her. To the *other* camp."

Theo didn't like the sound of that one bit.

CHAPTER
NINETEEN

Theo clung to the edge of the firelight. She watched as Alexander laughed and ate s'mores, watched as Wil talked to Edgar and the other counselors without ever once looking down and getting lost in her phone.

She wondered when she became the Sinister-Winterbottom who couldn't fit in at camp.

She wondered if maybe they'd all be better off if she went into the tie-dye room without the magnifying glass and the stopwatch. Could something like that really change her brain? Or did it just give Alexander and Wil the permission they needed to blend in, to join the group, to relax?

Maybe all this time they'd been making themselves unhappy, running around, looking for mysteries so they'd have something to focus on besides missing their parents. Maybe their parents really had decided to take the summer off. Theo had been told she was exhausting. Never by her parents, but what if they felt that way, too? What if they needed a break . . . from her?

What if the room didn't change brains at all? If *everyone* noticed the words and messages, and didn't think they were a threat? What if Wil and Alexander had gotten to this camp and realized they had a chance to have fun, and they were taking it, and Theo was going to be left out because she couldn't accept that things were okay? Because she couldn't stop the hive of bees in her chest from making her act out so she could quiet that buzzing?

She had thought she was the most suited to camp, but maybe she had been wrong. Was *she* the weird kid crawling under a building, hiding from a normal, fun summer?

Theo made her way over and sat next to Alexander. He smiled at her, then went back to his boondoggle. He was already an inch in, carefully weaving the fluorescent plastic threads in their pattern.

"Nice," Theo said.

"Thanks! I think so, too!"

"I wish these were deconstructed s'mores," Theo said, referencing Alexander's amazing invention that he had debuted at the Sanguine Spa. "Though I really don't want to eat any more marshmallows after our rabies decoy."

"Regular s'mores are the best kind! I like regular everything."

Alexander didn't like regular things. But she wasn't here to argue about s'mores. Theo leaned closer, lowering her voice. "Have you been able to snoop? What happened at dinner? I missed it."

"Oh, it was great! There were corn dogs and tater tots and everything was lukewarm and I'm not sure how long it was sitting out, but there sure was a lot of it!"

"A lukewarm buffet food service? Are you okay?" Theo had watched Alexander only eat fruit rather than risk contaminated food. He always said *buffet* and *no way* rhymed for a reason. And that reason definitely wasn't spelling, because it made no sense for them to rhyme based on how they were spelled.

"Yeah! There was juice, too, and chocolate milk."

"What about the food-safety protocols?"

Alexander shrugged. "It's not my job to worry about those. It's my job to have the best summer for every kid."

"Well, I found some stuff. Do you want to know what I found?" The book was digging into her stomach under her shirt.

Alexander shrugged again, eyes on his boondoggle. "If you want to tell me, I guess."

"Don't you care? About all the mysteries? About why we came here?"

Alexander met her gaze, the flickering fire reflected in his eyes, so they didn't look the same color as her own anymore. "We came here to have the best summer for every kid. Mysteries aren't on the schedule. The schedule is fun. Besides, mysteries aren't really my thing. I like sports."

Theo gasped in shock. "You do not."

"I do."

"Name one sport you like!"

"I can't."

Theo was about to crow triumphantly when Alexander continued. "I can't name only one, because I like them all. All the most popular sports."

"They stole your book!" Theo blurted, trying to say something, anything that would get a normal reaction.

"My book?" Alexander frowned, as though trying to

remember. Then he shrugged. "Well, it's summertime. No kids read for fun during the summer."

"That boondoggle's looking great, Alex!" Ricky said, giving him a thumbs-up from a couple seats away.

"Actually, it's Alexander," Theo said.

Alexander went back to looking at his boondoggle. "That's all right. I don't mind *Alex*."

Theo went cold in spite of the fire. "Yes, you do."

"No, I don't. *Alex* is much more common. Besides, *Alexander* is a lot of syllables to expect someone to use. What an inconvenience!"

"Your name isn't an inconvenience!"

"I don't mind. You can start calling me Alex like everyone else, too. It's nice to do what everyone else does."

Theo couldn't take this anymore. She stalked off into the darkness, and Alexander didn't even call to her to be careful, or to take a light, or to advise her on which animals might be lurking outside at night in this region. Theo found a quiet spot next to a cabin and sat on the ground with her back against the wall. She wrapped her arms around her legs, hugging her knees to her chest.

That wasn't Alexander.

Not really.

She had always wanted him to take things a little less seriously, to be able to have more fun, but not like that. This wasn't some version of Alexander that had always been there, waiting to break free as he mastered his fears and anxieties. This was a version where everything that made Alexander special, extraordinary, unique, *himself* was pushed down, hidden, pretended away. Made to fit whatever was easiest for other people to deal with. So that he'd be the most convenient twelve-year-old for a place like this.

Theo wanted to burst into the office and demand answers, to go back to the tie-dye hut and tear it apart. But if she acted out, they'd send her to the other camp she'd heard Dr. Jay mention. She'd be separated from Alexander now that he needed her the most. Or rather, now that he seemed not to need her at all.

But that made her certain he needed her more than ever. Now she not only had to be brave for both of them, she also had to be cautious for both of them. Because their mother's letter had told her to be brave and Alexander to be cautious, but if they had taken away what made Alexander Alexander, then he wouldn't be cautious anymore. She'd have to do it.

And Wil wasn't even using her phone like the letter said to! Theo couldn't exactly do that for her.

She had to fix this, and she had to fix this fast. It was all up to Theo.

But where to start? Certainly not with any of the counselors. They were useless. No, the only person who could give her answers was the only other person who didn't fit in here at all.

"Henry," Theo said aloud.

"What?" a voice answered from beneath the cabin next to her.

CHAPTER
TWENTY

"There you are!" Theo wriggled underneath the cabin. Theo didn't know why the cabins were built to sit up off the ground. She didn't worry about things like that, which made her sad, because Alexander definitely did worry about things like that. Or, at least, he *should* worry about it. He would have been able to tell her why the cabins were built this way, and also what types of spiders and other venomous creepy-crawlies would make homes down here, and also what would happen if the support beams failed and the cabin dropped on top of her.

She needed Alexander back. How else could she know all the things in the world to worry over and then make informed decisions about whether or not to care?

"You're still you," Henry said. He didn't sound happy about it. But he had a voice like a scowl, so he never sounded happy about anything. Theo wondered if his unpleasant voice came first and made him sound unpleasant, so everything became unpleasant, or if he treated everything as unpleasant and so his voice grew to reflect that.

"Yeah. I figured out how to see the messages." Wait—someone had left her those purple glasses. Would they have blocked the messages, too? "Did you leave me glasses?"

"I don't wear glasses! Are you calling me a nerd?" When Henry used exclamation marks, it was not because of enthusiasm. He sounded like he was on the verge of challenging her to a duel.

"No. And also wearing glasses doesn't make someone a nerd. Thinking wearing glasses makes someone a nerd is what makes someone a nerd."

"Wait—are you calling me a nerd *now?*"

Theo let Henry stew over it, while she puzzled over

who would have left the glasses if not him. Was Edgaren't here, trying to trick her? Or the fake Mrs. Widow? Where the glasses came from was her least-pressing problem, though.

"They got my brother," Theo said. "The tie-dye cult."

Henry let an annoyed growl out. "Brainwashing."

"More like braindyeing," Theo said. The ideas soaked in and colored over whatever your brain used to be so all that was left was swirling, happy colors. "How can I fix him?"

"It wears off at first. She starts it with the dye and the room, but she keeps it up with something else. I'm not sure what. I avoid her at all costs so I don't find out."

"The bell!" That weird music tone that had played and made Heidi and Ricky freeze and had lulled them all during mandatory rest time. It must be the exact same one that was played during the tie-dye sessions. Theo bet it was what they were listening to on their headphones at night, too.

"I hate that noise!" Henry punched the wooden floor planks above them, then said an alarmingly impolite word as he cradled his hurt hand. "Maybe that's why it didn't work on me. The noise made me so angry I threw all the dye and ran out. My aunt hates my temper. She tells me it's a terrible trait and I should never be angry about anything, ever."

"What kind of doctor is she? Some sort of mad scientist? Corrupted therapist?"

"She has a PhD in color theory as applied to advertising."

"*What?*"

"Are you calling me a liar?"

"No, but that's . . . that's ridiculous."

"No one used to call her Dr. Jay. Her name is Lily Jecky. But when she took over, she demanded everyone call her Dr. Jay."

"What do you mean took over?"

"This was my family's camp. But my dad—" His voice caught, and for a second, he sounded sad. Then he growled again. "My stupid dad left, and my aunt took it over and made it into Camp Creek. It hasn't been the same since."

"Your dad is gone?" But the name Jecky hadn't been on any of the books from the Sanguine Spa. So surely Henry's dad wasn't part of the same problem that Theo and Alexander's, Mina and Lucy's, and Edgar's parents might be caught up in.

"Yeah, so? Parents leave sometimes!"

Theo sighed. "I know. Believe me."

"You can't make me believe you! I don't have to do anything I don't want to!"

"Henry!" Theo resisted the urge to throw a handful of dirt at him. "All I need to know is how to undo the braindyeing!"

"If I knew, would I be down here? The more dye sessions someone goes to, the harder it is to snap them out of it. Until eventually it becomes . . . permanent."

Theo wasn't about to let that happen. She was going to get Alexander back, no matter what. But in order to do that, she'd have to make sure she wasn't sent to the other camp. It sounded ominous, a fancy word for intimidatingly scary. Alexander had taught it to her. He knew many, many words to describe things as scary.

In order to avoid the ominous other camp, Theo was going to have to fit in at this one. Which shouldn't have been a problem. She'd had no problems on the first day, since she already loved most of the activities here. But she'd have to follow all the rules, and smile when she didn't feel like it, and pretend like she didn't care about winning, and act like she wasn't a person made up of a hive of bees, ready to swarm out of control when things got too big or confusing or boring.

In short, she'd have to be the version of herself that her parents assured her they weren't interested in but some other adults and her one terrible teacher had always insisted she should be.

Theo could do this, though. She had to. She would pretend to be Dr. Jay's idea of *normal* long enough to save Alexander, and then, with his help, save Wil and Edgar, and then, with their help, find the missing books and figure out where their parents were.

"I'm going to fight them," Theo said, determined.

"How?" Henry asked doubtfully.

"By pretending to be exactly what they want me to be. Like a secret agent. Will you help me?"

"Definitely not! I don't owe you anything! I'm looking out for myself!"

"But if we beat them, then—" Theo stopped talking. "Henry?" There was no answer. Henry was gone, once again. "How does he keep doing that?" she grumbled as she crawled back out from under the cabin.

It was too late to convince Dr. Jay that today's session had worked, so Theo would have to show up at the tie-dye cabin first thing in the morning. The idea of returning to that swirling room made Theo feel sick to her stomach. That, or her stomach hurt from skipping dinner. So she went back to the bonfire with Alexander and Quincy and ate s'mores until her stomach hurt from too many s'mores instead of being worried.

That night, after brushing their teeth, everyone went immediately to bed and fell asleep instantly, headphones in place. Theo waited until Alexander was fully asleep, then hung down from the top bunk and carefully shifted his headphones so they weren't over his ears. At least that way he'd have a night free from that terrible tone telling him to be normal.

Theo lay wide awake and fuming and desperately missing her brother. It was lonely, plotting to overthrow a camp all by herself. She didn't know if any of her plans were good, if they were reckful or merely reckless, because she didn't have Alexander's caution to balance her bravery. And she didn't know if there was information she should have but didn't, especially about Dr. Jay, because Wil didn't have Rodrigo handy to look things up.

Theo had never really been on her own, and she didn't like it one bit. The Sinister-Winterbottoms were a team. They always had been. Thanks to this horrid braindyeing camp, Theo no longer had her team.

She sat up in bed and looked over at where Quincy

was asleep, lying flat on her back instead of curled in a hammock made of lassos. Even with Alexander no longer Alexander, Theo could still imagine what he would say about their former friend.

Alexander felt so many things all the time, he was good at understanding what other people might be feeling. And he'd probably tell Theo that Quincy didn't have anyone except terrible Edgaren't. And maybe . . . maybe there was a reason why Quincy had been helping Edgaren't. After all, Quincy didn't have a team like the Sinister-Winterbottoms. She was on her own. Theo hadn't been able to understand that before, but now she almost could.

Theo glared and stuck out her tongue. Quincy was still a traitor, and Theo didn't want to stop being mad. Imaginary Alexander in her head could put a sock in it. Until he was back to himself, she didn't have to listen to him.

But she still couldn't sleep. Letting out a frustrated huff, she climbed down and crossed the floor to Quincy's bottom bunk.

"I'm just doing this so you'll go back to yourself and I can make you give me answers," Theo hissed, moving Quincy's headphones, too. It definitely wasn't because she cared about her former friend, or missed Quincy's stupid rope tricks or the way her cowgirl hat made her ears stick out in a cute way, or was willing to forgive her.

Theo settled back down yet again and pulled out Alexander's book. It was long and not a subject she was interested in, but she started reading anyway. It started in the far-distant past, talking about the types of animals that roamed this region long before humans. It didn't seem important, but she didn't want to skip anything and risk losing vital information.

Eventually, her mind drifting and her eyes drooping, she gave up. She'd read more when she could. Theo pulled out her timer and wound it, letting the ticking noise soothe her as she tried to sleep. She'd need rest if she was going to pull off the biggest trick of her life the next day.

It was a good thing she was competitive. Because in the morning, Theo Sinister-Winterbottom was going to be the best, most aggressively boring and normal child this camp had ever seen.

CHAPTER
TWENTY-ONE

As soon as the morning braindyeing tone rang out, Theo leaped out of bed. All the other kids sat up in unison, stretching and smiling.

"Ready for another great day at camp?" Alexander asked.

"I sure am!" Theo answered. "But first, I'm going back to the tie-dye cabin. My shirt yesterday didn't turn out, and I really want to fit in!" She did her best to fake a smile for the person who was not quite her brother.

He smiled back. "Have fun!"

"Oh, I will." Theo clenched her fists and stomped

down the path. It was still early morning, the sun filtering through the trees in shafts of golden light. Everything smelled fresh and invigorating. It really was a beautiful camp, the perfect location, with cozy cabins and an amazing lake and tons of fun activities.

Theo was going to destroy it all if she had her way.

Dr. Jay opened the door to the dyeing cabin after Theo's third insistent knock. She wasn't even swathed in her tie-dyed robes yet, wearing a simple white lab coat with *JECKY, L. L.* embroidered over her heart. "Yes?" she asked.

"I want to try again," Theo said, which was the truth. "I feel—I feel left out, and sad, and—" What had Henry said his aunt hated? "And angry," Theo added, which was also the truth. Her parents always told her that anything she felt was valid, and she was allowed to feel all her feelings. They helped her figure out how to feel them in ways that weren't destructive and didn't hurt other people. That seemed much healthier than saying a whole category of feelings wasn't allowed.

Dr. Jay didn't share her parents' philosophy of feelings. "Oh, no, anger is terrible and should be avoided at all costs. And you should *never* be sad. We'll get you blending right in." She stepped aside to let Theo in, patting her shoulder in a stiff, awkward way that was supposed to be comforting. "You're exactly the type of child Camp Creek is made for. And we're going to make you exactly the type of child you should be."

Theo sat in her seat, trying to figure out the right amount of fidgeting to do in order to be convincing that she was still herself but didn't want to be anymore. Dr. Jay set her up with a shirt and the dyes, then backed out of the room with her oatmeal smile.

Theo reached into her shirt and pulled out her timer, winding it and resting it on her shoulder next to her ear. The room began to spin with the words telling Theo how she should be. Then the terrible tone with its secret messages began to play, but Theo kept her eyes down and her mind on the *tick-tick-tick* of her stopwatch.

Taking a deep breath, Theo picked up the first bottle of dye and got to work. By the time the room stopped spinning, Theo had created a tie-dye masterpiece. Her shirt looked like a rainbow had gotten in a fistfight with a unicorn. Theo just had time to hide her timer again and tuck something else in her pocket before Dr. Jay came back into the room, now wearing her own tie-dyed ensemble.

"That's much better!" Dr. Jay said, holding up Theo's shirt.

Theo gave her biggest, blandest smile. "Thank you! I feel really happy!"

Dr. Jay leaned closer, examining Theo's face. Theo did her best to hold on to that smile like a shield to protect herself from really being seen. Dr. Jay nodded, satisfied. "There's a good girl. Sit here and listen to the music while I get this rinsed and dried."

Theo wanted to fidget. She wanted to run around the room, tearing down the cloth draping every surface. She wanted to roll her eyes or sing at the top of her lungs to drown out the terrible music that wasn't music at all.

Instead she sat, perfectly still, smiling blankly.

"Here we are!" Dr. Jay said, coming back in after an agonizingly long wait. She handed Theo her new shirt. Theo immediately pulled it over her own T-shirt, looking down and smiling.

"Wow! This is great! Can I go to breakfast now, please? I can't wait for the cereal choices!"

"Of course." Dr. Jay opened the door, and Theo walked calmly out into the sunshine, then headed straight for the lodge. She walked like she was supposed to—with soft, even steps, no stomping or marching or sprinting.

When she reached the cafeteria, she joined the line without looking for Alexander to sit by, because everyone here was her friend now.

There was, in fact, a lot of cereal. So, so much cereal.

"Wow!" Theo said, her teeth gritted in her fake smile. "I can't believe it!"

"I know!" a voice said behind her. Theo turned to see Heidi and Ricky. They were standing with Wil and Edgar, all of them smiling, smiling, smiling.

"I think I'll mix two of them, like you do, Heidi!" Theo said.

Heidi's smile got even bigger. "It's so much fun!"

"The funnest!" Theo glanced at Wil and Edgar, but their smiles hadn't budged.

"I'm so glad you're having fun!" Wil said.

"And fitting right in!" Edgar added.

"I'm so glad, too!" Theo filled her cereal bowl, then sat down at the nearest table, trying not to slam her bowl down or eat too fast or glare in annoyance when Quincy sat across from her.

"I don't even like cereal," Quincy said with a smile, shoveling it into her mouth. "But I guess I do!"

"I guess so!" Theo answered, eating hers aggressively, then reminding herself that she was *happy* and *normal*.

"Every time I look at you, I feel like I need to be doing something, but I can't remember what," Quincy said, and her smile dropped a little bit, a flicker of confusion on her face like a candle about to sputter out.

"Probably betraying me," Theo said, still smiling.

"What?" Quincy asked.

"I said, probably returning your tray!" Theo pointed at Quincy's tray beneath her cereal bowl. "Can't leave it out on the table once you're done!"

Quincy looked down and nodded, smiling once more. "You're right!"

"I sure am!" Theo finished shoveling in her cereal, then returned her own tray. She kept an eye on Alexander at all times, watching as he smiled and ate next to perfect strangers. She wished she could talk to him, or drag him out and wash his brain in the lake, even if there were amoebas waiting to eat it.

What was he thinking right now?

CHAPTER
TWENTY-TWO

Normal normal normal, the tone in Alexander's head played as he ate his cereal. Something about this room bothered him, something here made him think—but there was all the tie-dye, a sea of it, and his eyes were soothed and distracted.

Normal normal normal, he thought without really thinking it as he worked on his boondoggle, his fingers busy doing nothing so that his brain didn't have to think or worry or generate any independent thought. Did he like doing this? It didn't matter. It was on the schedule, and the schedule was fun, and so this was fun.

Normal normal normal, he thought as he climbed the ladder to the rope swing. Something deep inside him seemed to want his attention, but the tone was playing in the background and in his head, promising him that *everything will be easy, everything will be simple, everything will be fun and good and normal normal normal.*

He saw his sister, and she was doing all the same things, the same things he was doing, the same things everyone was doing, they were all doing the same things and thinking the same things and feeling the same things and everything was normal normal normal, and this was the summer every child should have, and he was having it, and he shouldn't think about anything else.

CHAPTER
TWENTY-THREE

The rope swing was thrilling, and paddling around in a canoe was delightful, and volleyball was one of her favorite sports, and archery was just plain awesome, and the climbing wall was challenging in the best way, and the zip line was perfectly zippy, and Theo was so, so mad.

She couldn't enjoy any of it, because she was too busy pretending to have exactly the right amount of fun to blend in, and also keeping an eye on Alexander to make sure he was safe enough now that he wasn't being cautious. Which was bananas! Theo had never in her life had to watch out for Alexander. It had always been the opposite.

His shoelaces weren't even double-knotted. What if they came undone while he was running and he tripped and fell and hit a rock wrong and knocked out a permanent tooth? What if they came undone and caught on the canoe as he was getting out and he flipped upside down underwater? What if—

She shook her head, trying to stop the parade of all the terrible things that might go wrong. It was stressful, and exhausting. No wonder Alexander needed to take breaks from activities even if he liked them.

On the archery range, Theo was the one who shouted—while smiling—any time another kid had their arrow nocked but wasn't paying enough attention where they were pointing it. She barely even noticed that she got three bull's-eyes herself. She definitely noticed Alexander's blank smile and glazed expression as he shot.

On the canoes, Theo was the one who shouted—while smiling—that Alexander had forgotten his life jacket and absolutely could not go paddling without one. She barely even noticed how satisfying it was to pull the paddle through the water and propel the canoe across the shining surface. She definitely noticed the small open shed on the other side of the lake, though, where canoes went to be repaired.

On the rope swing, Theo was the one who shouted—while smiling—that the next person up needed to make certain the person before them had swum clear of the landing area before swinging out. She barely even noticed the exhilaration of a perfectly timed swing and release and refreshing plunge into the chilly lake water. She definitely noticed the way Quincy paused, the rope in her hands, looking at it like she was remembering something before the lifeguard shouted that it was her turn.

On the volleyball court, Theo was the one who shouted—without smiling—that she was going to destroy the other team so completely they would never be able to show their faces on a volleyball court ever again, because volleyballs would instantly deflate in shame and nets would shrivel rather than letting such a terrible team touch them!

Theo cleared her throat after that one, putting on another fake smile. "Just kidding!" she said. "This is so fun!" But it wasn't, because she had to work so hard to be normal at volleyball. It was the same with the climbing wall. Theo wanted to scramble to the top as fast as she could, but all the other kids were taking their time, smiling, waving to each other. Even lunch pushed Theo to her limits, sitting and calmly eating, like the soggy chicken nuggets

173

were worth lingering over when there was so much to do outside.

It turned out it was as exhausting trying to be like everyone else as it was trying to be extra cautious.

But Theo *had* to be careful. Heidi and Ricky and the other counselors were always close by. Any time it looked like Theo might be getting tired, or not having fun, or even thinking about sneaking off to be sneaky, they would jump in.

"Let's play a game!" Heidi would say.

"We love games!" Ricky would add.

"Games are the best!" another counselor would jump in, so on and so forth, until they had all established that they really, absolutely, definitely, *super* loved games. Theo played clapping games, ball games, throwing games, swimming games, and board games, all while feeling like she was playing mind games.

She didn't have a moment to herself. All her attempts to lure Alexander away from the group were immediately thwarted. She was getting impatient, which made it harder and harder to smile and pretend like she was having a good time. Her brother wasn't due back in the braindyeing cabin that day, which was a relief. But they were coming up on the afternoon mandatory rest time.

That tone would blare, making sure the braindye was still soaking in nice and deep. Making sure Camp Creek Alexander stayed while the real Alexander slipped further away.

Theo couldn't stand it. It was time to quit hoping for a chance to steal him away and to *make* her chance instead.

While they were playing hot potato with a water balloon, everyone grinning and smiling and smiling and grinning, Theo slipped her hand into her pocket and pulled out what she had stolen from Dr. Jay: one bottle of concentrated red dye.

Theo knew if Alexander and Wil and Edgar were themselves, they'd never believe what was about to happen. But none of them were themselves. Yet. Theo leaped to catch the water balloon, then tripped on nothing, exaggeratedly pinwheeling her arms. "Oh no!" she shouted. "I'm falling!" She fell to the ground, covering the dye bottle with her hand.

"Yikes!" Heidi said.

"I hope you're okay!" Ricky said.

"I don't think I am!" Theo said, grinning as she held up her hand, now absolutely covered in dripping red dye.

Alexander didn't panic. He didn't immediately tell her all about first aid and the exact order they should do things to take care of her hand. He didn't groan that he knew this would happen, playing such a rough game on uneven ground. He just stared at her hand, not smiling, not frowning. The braindyed version of Alexander didn't have a response to something so un-fun, something so out of the ordinary. He was broken.

Everyone else was, too. They all stared, their faces wanting to smile, but what was left of their brains knowing that smiling wasn't okay right now.

"I'll go find Dr. Jay." Theo held her hand against her chest in case anyone was looking closely for a wound that didn't exist.

"Great idea!" Ricky said, a relieved smile popping back onto his face.

"Way to go!" Heidi, too, smiled in relief. "You're so smart!"

"I think we have our camper of the day!" Edgar said. "Along with every other camper, too, of course! Wouldn't want to leave anyone out! We all have to stick together!"

"Yeah! I'm definitely not at all concerned about this or what she's doing!" Wil said, watching Theo with wide eyes.

"Don't wait for me," Theo said. "Go ahead and keep playing!" Theo walked at a happy, reasonable pace down the path that would take her to Dr. Jay's creepy dye cabin. As soon as she was out of view of the counselors, she cut through the trees back to the office.

She tapped lightly on the window. If someone came to see who was knocking, she had her excuse that she was bleeding and got confused. But no one answered.

And, even better, Theo's trick of nearly-but-not-quite closing the window last night had worked. It wasn't latched. There was a hose spigot back here, so she used it to rinse off as much of the dye as she could, lest she be caught literally red-handed. Then she eased up the window and climbed in, immediately going to work on the drawer with Quincy's lassos.

She felt like a ninja, or a secret agent, but no one was here to appreciate it. It was a very sad thing, doing something so cool without anyone knowing. Alexander would have had some goofy pun right about now. And he also would have been practically melting with panic.

Theo popped the drawers open in record time. She took the ropes and wrapped them around her waist, hidden beneath her big tie-dyed shirt. Then, since she was stealing things anyway, she took their mother's letter, putting it in her pocket. Back out the window, a quick stop at one of the restrooms that were clean but always seemed to have exactly one bee inside, and she was ready.

She skipped to the group, a wad of toilet paper wrapped around her hand. "All better!" she said.

"Yay!" everyone cheered in unison. Alexander didn't ask about how they had cleaned the wound, whether the dressing was protective enough, and what they would do to prevent infection and promote healing. He only smiled, flashing her a thumbs-up.

"You're back just in time!" Heidi said, clapping her hands together.

"I can't believe it's time already!" Wil said, beaming.

"I love mandatory rest time!" Edgar's smile gleamed in the brilliant summer sun.

"Me too!" Ricky said.

"Me three!" Georgie added.

Theo wanted to scream as every single other counselor continued to add themselves with *me four, me five,* on and on up to *me ten.*

But once they had all chimed in with how much they absolutely loved being forced to lie still in bed for an hour during the day—which Theo could not possibly believe anyone would want to do—it was time to get to their bunks.

Theo buzzed with anticipation. This was it. This was where her plan went into action. She walked right behind Alexander, watching the back of his head. "Excited for mandatory rest time, Alex?" another camper asked.

"He doesn't like being called Alex," a voice said next to Theo.

She turned, startled, to see Quincy walking next to her. Quincy was frowning, ever so slightly.

"No, he doesn't," Theo said, wary. Maybe this was a trick. Or maybe removing their headphones last night had helped a little.

"How do I know that?" Quincy looked over at Theo, and even though her smile came back into place, it wobbled like the watery strawberry gelatin they had eaten for dessert with lunch. "And why do I feel like crying every time I look at you?"

"Quincy!" Heidi said. "You look sad!"

"She's not sad!" Theo blurted. "We're planning a game for later! It's a surprise!"

"Oh! I love games! And surprises!" Heidi held the door to the cabin open. She and Ricky watched as everyone lay down. Theo hesitated.

Alexander's bunk was right below hers. And Quincy's was across the room. Quincy wasn't part of this plan. She didn't deserve to be. If Quincy's brain had been dyed, well, that was good! Theo didn't like Quincy's traitor brain!

But. Quincy had looked so sad for a moment there. And she stuck up for Alexander even when she didn't remember why she was doing it.

Sighing in annoyance, Theo lay down on her bed and closed her eyes. The tone started. Everyone in the cabin around her was absolutely silent and still, letting the dye continue to soak into their brains, changing everything about them. Accompanied by the ticking of her timer, Theo crept out of bed, grabbed Alexander's book from under her pillow, and then fastened the recovered ropes into two perfect lassos.

It was time to steal her brother *and* her former friend back.

CHAPTER
TWENTY-FOUR

"But what are we doing under this canoe?" Alexander asked, smiling.

"We're playing a game," Theo snapped. It had been hard work, lassoing Alexander and Quincy, dragging them out of their beds, across the floor, and out of the cabin. No one had even noticed, thanks to Dr. Jay and her terrible "music." Even Alexander and Quincy hadn't reacted, flopping along the floor like two possums playing dead.

Theo was strong, but dragging two kids her own size was no joke. Fortunately, she wasn't far from the lakeshore, and she had been able to load them into a canoe—putting life jackets on both of them, even if

Alexander wasn't able to demand it—and then row them across the lake to the canoe repair area before the end of mandatory rest time.

Now they were all sitting underneath an overturned canoe. No one could see them, but Theo could still peer out and make sure they weren't about to be discovered.

"I love games!" Quincy said automatically.

"It's great that you're participating in group activities," Alexander said.

"It's healthy to be part of a group," Quincy agreed.

"But maybe we should go find the others." Though Alexander was still smiling, there was a hint of worry in his voice that gave Theo hope. "I don't think this was on the schedule."

Alexander worrying about not following the schedule was the first sign of success Theo had seen in the hour they'd been sitting there. "Oh, it's definitely not on the schedule." Theo smiled, and it wasn't a fake one at all. She turned to the next page in her book, which was still talking about the Ice Age and how it reformed the mountainous lake region.

After a couple more hours, Theo was through the Ice Age at last. It was harder to focus, though. They could hear the sounds of voices drifting through the trees, calling their names in chipper tones. "Quincy! Theo! Alex!"

Alexander's face twitched. "That's my name they're calling," he said, but he sounded unsure. Then his smile popped back into place. "We should answer them!"

"Nope," Theo said. "That's breaking the rules of our game. You wouldn't want to be a poor sport, would you?"

Alexander shook his head hurriedly. Theo leaned down and untied his shoelaces.

"I might trip," he said, and there! A flash of frown in place of an empty smile.

"You sure might!"

Quincy was distracted. She stared at the rope tied around them, securing her to Alexander. "I like these knots," she said. "Why do I like these knots?" She shook her head as though trying to get rid of a fly buzzing by her ears. "It's weird to like rope. I don't like rope, unless it's a swing. I like normal things! I like . . . golf. I like golf?" Quincy's hands twitched, reaching up to touch the rope. Not to undo it, but to run her fingers along the coils. "I like normal things," she whispered, but she sounded unsure.

Theo knew she needed to be patient. It was definitely

not a skill she had. And, unlike lockpicking, it was not a skill she wanted to learn. But she had to wait it out. She had to give Alexander's and Quincy's brains a chance to wash themselves free of the dye. So she kept reading.

It was a miserable slog of an endless summer afternoon. The canoe blocked any breeze, so it was muggy and hot. The ground beneath them was close enough to the lake that it was soggy, and before long, their shorts had soaked through. It was one thing to be wet on purpose, like going swimming, or playing in the rain, or finding a secret chamber behind a wave pool.

It was quite another thing to have to sit in wet shorts, tied up, with no breeze and no games and nothing to do.

But the more miserable things got, the more Alexander and Quincy began to look like themselves. Quincy's blank smile was slowly shifting into a scowl. Alexander's bright, happy face was pinching with worry, and he began twitching at random.

"Did you feel that?" he said, his smile flickering like his face was glitching. "Are we sure there aren't any venomous insects down here? This seems like a prime breeding ground for spiders and centipedes. Or slugs. I really don't want to meet any slugs under here." He looked around, worried, but still trying to smile.

"Oh, there are definitely slugs." Theo turned the page.

Under the canoe was all tie and no dye. Without the distraction of constant busyness, the oversight of their counselors, and the terrible music playing to keep soaking their brains in Dr. Jay's ideas of how children should feel and behave, whatever had been done to Alexander and Quincy was washing away. Much like they wished they could wash their muddy, sodden clothes.

Theo sighed. "I wish I was a faster reader. I've been reading for ages, and I'm still not up to the modern history of the region. But this part was interesting! Did you know this whole area was once dominated by giant, prehistoric burrowing ground sloths? Imagine that! Listen to this paragraph, *Alex*," Theo said.

"That's not my name," Alexander snapped.

Theo looked up, surprised. Alexander met her eyes, and there wasn't a hint of a smile on his face. "Theo," he said, "I don't know what's going on, but I feel like I've been eating in a buffet-style cafeteria, and I smell like bacteria-filled lake water, and my shoelaces aren't double-knotted, and I'm almost certain a slug has climbed up my shorts. If you don't untie me and let me check, I'm going to start screaming and I don't think I'll be able to stop."

"Alexander!" Theo threw her arms around her brother.

She felt tears pricking at her eyes, and she hastily wiped them away as she untied him.

"That was some excellent lassoing," Quincy said, her unique Texas drawl back in place. She was staring at the ground, eyes pooling with the same tears Theo had refused to let fall. "Theo, I—"

"Slug check first, talk after!" Alexander squeaked. He felt like he was waking up, like he had been sleepwalking through a strange and terrible dream. But the worst part was, it hadn't all been terrible. A lot of it had been really easy. Simple. He did as he was told, and he participated, and he didn't worry or question or stand out. He had literally been like everyone else.

But before he could wonder if maybe he had liked that part, he remembered standing in the food line behind a kid who kept wiping his nose and then reaching in to scoop out lukewarm, soggy chicken nuggets with his bare hands.

"This place is my worst nightmare." Alexander shuddered as Theo finished untying him. He stood, bonking his head against the top of the canoe, and did a dance known as the slug-in-my-shorts. It was briefly popular during the 1970s, but Alexander put all the other dancers to shame with his moves. At last satisfied that his shorts were slug-free, he went to sit again. But the dirt was muddy and churned up. It could be hiding anything. He stared down, unwilling to risk it.

Theo was still wearing her regular shirt underneath her tie-dyed one, so she peeled off the neon monstrosity and set it on the ground for Alexander to sit on.

"Thank you," he said, closing his eyes in relief. And also closing them because he didn't want to look around the canoe and check for other creepy-crawlies. For once, he'd rather not know. "What happened?" he asked, focusing on retying his shoelaces.

"You were braindyed." Theo watched Alexander and Quincy. Quincy had already undone the knots holding her in place, but she didn't shrug out of the ropes or try to get away.

"Don't you mean *brainwashed?*" Alexander asked.

"No, I washed your brains out under here. You were braindyed in that creepy cabin of Dr. Jay's. It's filled with subliminal messages. So is that terrible bell tone she plays all the time."

"But you weren't braindyed?" Quincy asked, her voice quiet, her eyes still firmly on the ground.

"No. I was able to block it with—" She caught herself. She wasn't going to tell Quincy about the magnifying glass or the timer, just in case. "Well, I figured out what was going on, so it didn't work on me. What do you remember?"

"Not much," Alexander said. "It's all a sort of blur. Like dye swirling around in water. Did I play *volleyball?*" He looked at Theo in shock. "Did I swim in a lake? Do you know what lake water is like? Do you know how many different things can make you sick if lake water goes through your nasal membranes?" He put his hands over his nose, pure terror in his eyes. "Tell me the truth: does it look like anything is eating my brain right now?"

Theo laughed, which made Alexander slump, hurt. She put her hands on his shoulders. "I'm not laughing at your fears! I mean, I am. But only because I'm relieved. It's exhausting having to worry about so many things. I did my best to be cautious since you were out of commission, but I was nowhere near as good at it as you are. I'm really, really glad to have you back." Theo hugged him again, even tighter. "I don't want you to change," she whispered. "Just in case you'd ever wondered if I'd like you better if you were different. I like you exactly how you are." She hadn't done a good enough job of letting him know that. And maybe sometimes she had wished he was different. But she knew now: she didn't want that.

Alexander closed his eyes, nodding against Theo's shoulder. He had, in fact, wondered that. Many times. One of his biggest, most terrible fears, the fear with the most teeth and the nastiest whispers, was that the people he loved would get tired of dealing with him. That they wished he was different. Easier. Their parents being gone had made that fear even worse, worrying that they had really only left because they needed a break from him.

But Theo *had* gotten a break from him. Alexander had been exactly like everyone else. And she had done all this to get him back the way he was before.

He'd had no idea how much he needed someone to tell him that it was okay to be himself. Maybe that's what their mother had been trying to say in her letter: that being cautious wasn't a flaw, or annoying, or a burden. It was part of who Alexander was, and she loved him, just like their dad loved him, just like Theo loved him. They didn't love him *in spite* of his constant anxieties and worries. He wasn't something that they put up with. They just loved him, period.

And he was pretty sure Wil did, too, but honestly, who knew with her.

"Wil!" Alexander said, pulling away. "Is she okay?"

Theo shook her head. "She and Edgar got braindyed, too. But I wanted to save you first."

"And me," Quincy said. "Why did you save me?" She looked up, the tears spilling from her eyes. "I don't deserve it."

Theo scowled at her. "Maybe not. But you didn't deserve to be whatever Dr. Jay wanted to make you, either. You didn't even tell a single person here you were from Texas."

Quincy's teary eyes widened in alarm. "I didn't?"

"Nope. And you didn't care that you didn't have your ropes."

Quincy had already managed to spool the ropes back up, twisting them around her hands without even thinking about it. "I can't believe he did this to me. To us."

"Edgaren't, you mean?"

Quincy frowned. "That's not his name. But yes. He promised me—he *promised*—that if I was good, that if I tried to be normal, that if I helped you out, too—that everything would be good again. He said he was helping your family."

"He's a liar! No one in my family would ever want or need his help."

"I see that now. I never meant to hurt you or to betray you. I promise. He made it sound like this was the only way to get your parents back, and I wanted that for you. For everyone."

"Really?" Theo demanded, narrowing her eyes.

Quincy nodded. "I swear it. On Texas."

Theo sighed. She still wanted to be mad, but she knew Quincy couldn't lie. Not when she was swearing on Texas. "I believe you. But it really hurt me when you turned us in. You were my friend."

"I'd still like to be."

Theo let out an aggravated huff. "I'd like you to be, too. But I still get to be mad."

"You can be mad as long as you need to be. I understand." Quincy definitely wasn't braindyed anymore. Dr. Jay didn't want anyone mad, ever, but good friends understand that sometimes people need to feel all the mad they have before they can accept, forgive, and move on.

"So Edgaren't definitely knows where our parents are?" Alexander asked. He had been hurt by Quincy, too, but he understood better than Theo did. Theo never cared what the adults in her life wanted her to do. Alexander *always* cared. If he had someone in his life like Edgaren't, bullying him, telling him to do things he suspected were wrong, he would probably listen, too. He didn't blame Quincy. And he was really glad they were back with her, and she was on their side now. Asking for forgiveness instead of giving up on being friends with them was super brave. No wonder Theo liked her.

Quincy shook her head. "I don't know if he knows where your parents are, but he definitely knows about them."

"Which means they probably aren't on a vacation." Alexander couldn't decide whether that was a relief or scarier than anything. "Which means we really need to get those books he stole and find some answers."

"Speaking of books." Theo held out the camp book, scowling. "I've been reading this all day, and it's useless. What good does it do us to know ancient burrowing giant ground sloths used to live here?"

"I can speed-read," Quincy offered. "I learned how to since I couldn't participate in speed-roping competitions, on account of being allergic to sheep. And cows. And dust." She sneezed right on cue. "May I?"

Theo handed the book over. Quincy began scanning the pages, almost impossibly fast. But she stopped halfway through. She looked up at the Sinister-Winterbottom twins in shock. "There's old camp photos in here," she said. "This is the lake, right?" She showed them the grainy black-and-white photo. The shoreline of the lake was unmistakable, complete with platform and rope swing.

"The rope swing is that old?" Alexander squeaked. "And I went on it?"

"Look." Quincy turned the page. There was a group photo of camp counselors, all wearing retro shirts and short shorts. Their arms were around each other's shoulders, and they were all smiling at the camera.

"I think that's my mom," Quincy said at the exact same time Theo and Alexander did, too.

CHAPTER
TWENTY-FIVE

"Your mom is our mom?" Theo asked, genuinely baffled.

Quincy pointed to a short teenage girl with long, straight hair done in two braids.

"Oh, that makes more sense. Except it doesn't make any sense. Because I'm pretty sure that's our mom," Theo pointed to a tall, freckled girl with her hair pushed back from her face by a headband. She was young—so young it kind of seemed impossible. Obviously, Alexander and Theo understood that their parents had not always been adults, but since they had only ever known their parents as adults, it was difficult to imagine them as anything else. The photo was blurry and the features weren't very distinct, but it looked similar enough to a photo of their mom as a teenager they had on the wall at home that they recognized her.

"So they came to this camp?" Alexander asked, squinting. "They knew each other then. Wait." Alexander always paid attention to details, to little things other people didn't notice. The phrase *don't sweat the small stuff* was not something he believed in. Small stuff was often worth sweating over. Ticks were small. Blood-borne infections were small. Slugs were not small enough, in his opinion, but were still relatively small.

But because Alexander very much sweated the small stuff, he noticed lots of details. He pointed to a tall young man with his arm around their mother. There was nothing particularly menacing about him, but something about his eyes made Alexander instantly feel nervous. "If you were to draw a large, mean mustache on that face . . ."

"Edgaren't!" Theo gasped. "What is he doing in a photo with our moms? I mean, I guess it makes sense with your mom, since he's your uncle."

"She never told me about summer camp. Or about my uncle, for that matter."

Alexander understood secret relatives. "Our mom never told us about summer camp, either. Or our aunt."

Aunt Saffronia was definitely not in the photo. But someone else they recognized was. "Look! What does her face remind you of?" He pointed to one of the teens.

"Absolutely nothing," Theo said. "I won't remember it as soon as I look away. That's gotta be Dr. Jay."

"Why is that guy covered in long sleeves and long pants and a huge hat and sunglasses and . . . is that a cape?" Quincy frowned. "Something about his smile is familiar, though. And that nose."

Alexander snapped his fingers. "I know who he is! Imagine him in a scary portrait, staring down at you from a painting that keeps changing!"

"Mr. Blood?" Theo could see it now that Alexander pointed it out. "So, Mina and Lucy's dad, our mom, your mom, Edgaren't, Dr. Jay . . . does that guy look a little like Edgar?" She pointed to a handsome young man whose uniform somehow looked a little neater than the others. He was holding a parasol to shade himself and the girl next to him.

"Could be. I don't know who any of these others are, though." There were several more teens, including an enormous boy with an oddly square head next to a skinny boy with a pointy chin; a squirrely-looking young woman who seemed like she had something up her sleeve (which was a difficult look to pull off with such short sleeves, but somehow she managed); a girl whose hair looked like a cartoon mermaid's, floating on wind that wasn't touching anyone else's hair; a boy who, unlike the others, was not smiling but rather looked deeply angry at being asked to pose for a photo; and Theo and Alexander's mother, standing on the edge of the group, looking blurry and indistinct.

"Wait!" they said at the same time.

"How is our mom in two places at once?" Alexander asked.

Theo shook her head. "Maybe the photo was edited?"

"Or maybe it's not her." Alexander practically had his nose against the page. "It's hard to make out any details on their faces."

"Does she have something in her hand?" Quincy asked. "I can't see well enough."

"I wish I had my—" Alexander started, but before he could finish, Theo whipped out his magnifying glass and passed it over. He smiled at her, then used it to get a closer look. Sure enough, the blurry girl on the end held this exact same magnifying glass in her hand.

"What the what?" Alexander whispered. He moved the glass over the photo. Around their mother's neck was Theo's timer. Edgaren't, with his arm around their mother's shoulder—the smiling one, not the blurry one who looked like her—had his fingers crossed. And what Alexander had originally taken to be a stack of firewood or something behind them was revealed to be a stack of books.

Familiar books.

"I think those are the books Edgaren't stole from the Sanguine Spa secret library!" he said, pointing excitedly. "So Edgaren't, and our mom, and Quincy's mom, and Dr. Jay, and probably one of Edgar's dads, and Mina and Lucy's dad were all at this camp together. They knew each other. They're all connected, somehow. And the girl on the end who looks like our mom has this magnifying glass. It has to mean something."

"Who were the campers that disappeared, though?" Theo asked.

Quincy took the book back, scanning the text. "It was from that group! Half the teen counselors just . . . disappeared. It was a huge mystery. They were in the middle of the summer season, and according to all the witnesses, everyone was having an awesome time. But then M. Graves—"

"My mom," Quincy whispered.

"R. Widow, V. Stein, M. Hyde, V. Blood, M. Siren, and . . . S. Sinister disappeared in the middle of the night."

"Both our moms," Quincy said.

"But they're not missing. Or, at least, they weren't missing for a long time. So does the book say they found them?"

Quincy flipped several pages, then shook her head. "It says they were never found. But it's an old book. Maybe it had already been printed by the time our parents were found or came back or whatever."

Theo held out her hands. "Give it here. There's an easy way to check when a book was printed." She took it and turned to the front. On a page near the beginning was always loads of information. The author, someone named Cal A. Mitty, whether the book was fiction or nonfiction, so on and so forth, including the printing date. "Huh." Theo frowned, doing the math in her head. "It was printed when our parents would have been, like, twenty. So they were still missing, four years later?"

"Or the author didn't bother following up. They just wanted to tell a scary story." Quincy took the book back, once again flipping to where they had been. "The only witness said she tried to stop them, but she couldn't. Her name was L. L. Jecky. Does that mean anything to either of you?"

"Dr. Jay!" Theo shouted, then lowered her voice. They were still hiding. She had almost forgotten, what with the excitement of these revelations, that they were underneath a canoe to avoid detection. The shouts for them were getting louder and closer. They were out of time. "It was on her coat. Dr. Jay is the only witness to whatever happened to our parents back then."

Alexander put his magnifying glass safely in his pocket, scowling and scratching the end of his freckled nose. "So she knows our moms and never said anything."

"We need answers," Theo said. "And Dr. Jay has them. But first things first." Theo tucked the camp history book back under her shirt. "We have to wash out Wil and Edgar's brains."

Quincy nodded, flicking the ropes expertly. "Let's go kidnap some counselors."

CHAPTER
TWENTY-SIX

Theo, Alexander, and Quincy emerged from under the canoe, bright-eyed and smiling.

"Hi!" Theo shouted, waving. A dozen counselors converged on them. All the counselors were smiling, maybe a little more intensely than their usual smiles. Which was saying something, because they were all intense smilers.

"We've been looking for you!" Heidi said.

"All over!" Ricky added.

"For hours!" Wil said, and it seemed like her smile was more gritted teeth than actual smiling.

"I know!" Alexander ignored that his shorts were wet. He ignored the creeping worry that he had spiderwebs in his hair, or that he had missed a slug in his clothes, or that he definitely hadn't checked how long lunch had been sitting in the food warmers, breeding bacteria. "We were playing hide-and-seek with you. We won! It's your turn to hide now!" He crossed his fingers behind his back that this would work. Their plan was to make the counselors hide, then find Wil and Edgar for a good brain wash.

"But that's not on the schedule!" Heidi said. She and Ricky and the other counselors surrounded Quincy, Theo, and Alexander, steering them back toward camp. "It's almost dark! That means it's campfire time!"

Theo and Alexander shared an urgent look. They had to keep the counselors distracted so they could isolate Edgar and Wil.

"But you love games," Theo said, trying her hardest to smile.

"Sure do!" Ricky said.

"Absolutely!" Heidi added.

"Oh, a hundred percent!" "Games are my favorite!" "Could play games all day!" chimed all around them.

"I have a game we can play at the bonfire!" Theo said, scrambling for a new plan. But the first game that came into her head was the worst, most aggravating, most impossible one she had ever played. A game that still nagged at her because she thought she had won, but she hadn't, and she had no way of ever winning now.

"Tell us!" Ricky said.

"It's a guessing game."

"Ooh! I love guessing! Seven! Purple! The Declaration of Independence! The freezing point of water!" Heidi began spurting things off at random.

Theo held up a hand to interrupt her. "The game is called What's My Sixth-Favorite Animal? You have to guess what my sixth-favorite animal is."

"What?" Quincy asked, aghast. *Aghast* was a similar feeling to surprised, as indicated by how close it is to saying, "A ghost!" which is always surprising. No one expects a ghost. Then Quincy caught herself and smiled. "I mean what! That's the best game ever! I love that game!"

"I've never heard of it!" Ricky said. "But I never say no to a group game! Campers, gather up! Georgie, go get the whiteboards!"

"I— But you need to just start guessing?" Theo was hoping they'd be so busy guessing they wouldn't notice her sneaking away. Instead, they sat her right down on a log next to a huge whiteboard with several markers. Heidi was already using it to create an elaborate bracket system for sorting and eliminating animals. Everyone gathered in front of Theo, making sneaking impossible.

"Let's set some ground rules!" Kiki said. She had appeared from the office, the lure of a new game too much for her to resist. "First of all, it has to be a real animal! Nothing mythological or fictional!"

A camper raised his hand. "Can it be extinct?"

"I don't know!" Kiki turned to Theo. Theo noticed that Wil and Edgar were hanging out at the back of the group. The day was quickly slipping into twilight, the air growing darker as the fire grew brighter. Theo jerked her head meaningfully toward Wil and Edgar. Alexander and Quincy nodded.

Alexander was nervous. Theo was supposed to be in charge of this part. But Theo was keeping all the other counselors busy. It was up to him and Quincy. He was glad Theo had been able to forgive Quincy, because the idea of any of this scared him, but the idea of doing it alone scared him even more.

Still. Wil needed their help, and Edgar needed to get out of those horrible clothes. Theo had saved Alexander and Quincy, so now they could save Wil and Edgar.

"Nothing extinct," Theo agreed. "Though I did learn about giant burrowing ground sloths today, and I like them a lot."

"Great!" Kiki erased an entire list of dinosaurs she had already been making. "Nothing extinct! That really narrows it down! Now! Tell us your favorite foods, books, movies, sports, colors, and the best present you ever got for your birthday!"

Alexander and Quincy left a puzzled-looking Theo. They crept backward, away from the group. It was easy, with everyone so incredibly intent on Theo's absurd game.

"What *is* her sixth-favorite animal?" Quincy whispered.

"I have no idea. I don't even know if *she* knows." Alexander didn't know what his own sixth-favorite animal was. He had a lot of rankings—top-ten things he'd never eat, top-ten worst ways he could get injured on the school playground, top-ten numbers one through ten (he was partial to three)—but he had never ranked his top-ten animals. He didn't want to think about any animals at all right now, creeping through the darkening forest with Quincy.

"This'll work." Quincy looked around with her hands

on her hips. The woods here got wild fast, the trees towering and ancient. They didn't have to go in very deep before it felt like camp had never existed at all.

"Wasn't Theo saying something about giant burrowing ground sloths?" Alexander asked, looking around nervously. He couldn't stop thinking about animals now that he had decided he didn't want to.

"Are those her sixth-favorite animal?" Quincy threw one of her ropes. It sailed upward, disappearing into the darkness.

"What? No. I think they're extinct. I hope they are, anyway." He couldn't get over the image of an enormous clawed sloth creeping up from behind them. Or beneath them, on account of the tunneling. He knew everyone thought sloths were cute, but he only had eyes for their enormous claws. If a regular sloth had giant claws, how much bigger would the claws on a giant sloth be?

"I wonder if I'd be allergic to them." Quincy stepped back and examined her work. "I think we're all set here."

Alexander left Quincy in the dark, glad that wasn't his role. He carefully made his way back to the firelight. The animal brackets were half-filled in now, the arguments around the rankings both enthusiastic and detailed.

"But since Theo has said she likes taking walks at

night, we can safely assume nocturnal animals will rank higher on the list!" Ricky said, gesturing to a whole section of them.

"That's true!" Heidi agreed. "But Theo also said her favorite weather is sunshine, so we can't eliminate the others just yet! And, given that Theo picked a sword over a shield when given the choice between the two, I think we should rank predators higher than non-predatory animals!"

"That's true!" Kiki agreed. "But remember, we're looking for her sixth favorite, not her first favorite, so we have to factor that in!"

Theo sat on her log, dazed, trying to smile as she followed the dizzying arguments. Alexander was in luck. Wil and Edgar were already separated from the group, stepping into the darkness.

"There you are!" Alexander whispered. "I have to show you something!"

"You don't!" Wil said, smiling in the darkness so her teeth glowed.

"You really don't!" Edgar agreed.

"You should get back to the game!" Wil insisted.

"It's a cell phone!" Alexander blurted. "I think someone snuck one in!"

Wil and Edgar looked at each other, then turned back to Alexander. "Okay, show us!" Wil said. She and Edgar followed Alexander into the darkness. For one panic-stricken moment, Alexander was certain he had lost his way and they'd walk right past Quincy and into the waiting arms of Dr. Jay, who would once again convince Alexander he liked volleyball and was not, in fact, deeply terrified of getting hit in the face. In terms of his sports-related fears, it ranked only slightly lower than the fear of getting bonked on the head with a stray golf ball, and just above the fear of somehow being chosen for a three-point shooting contest in front of an entire arena of sports fans.

Alexander heard a whistle and corrected course. Good old Quincy.

She appeared from behind a tree. "Howdy!" she said brightly. Then she tugged on a rope. The loops hidden under leaves right where Wil and Edgar were standing snapped tight, tugging their legs out from under them so they dangled upside down in the air, suspended from Quincy's ropes, which were suspended from tree branches in an elaborate system that Alexander didn't understand but definitely admired.

"What are you doing?!" Wil hissed.

"I'm sorry," Alexander said, "but you've been brainwashed. I mean braindyed. Theo saved us, and this is the only way to save you."

Wil folded her arms, and even though it was dark, Alexander could sense that Wil definitely, absolutely, totally, was *not smiling.*

"Why do you twerps keep assuming that I need to be saved?" she said.

CHAPTER
TWENTY-SEVEN

Wil and Edgar were swaying slightly in the night breeze, suspended upside down from a tree, and Wil was not happy about it. Which meant that she was not smiling. Which meant ...

"Wait, you aren't braindyed?" Alexander asked.

"No, I'm not braindyed!" Wil might have said it with an exclamation mark, but it wasn't a happy one.

"I'm not, either," Edgar said, sounding vaguely apologetic about it. "Though I do admire and appreciate the effort you've both put in here."

"But you *were* braindyed?" Wil was definitely upset. "We left those glasses for both of you to use so it wouldn't affect you. And we told you to have fun, meaning play along. I thought you were faking it!" She paused. "I guess I should have known when you ate from the buffet."

Alexander shuddered. "Please don't remind me. And I don't know anything about glasses. I never saw them. Theo managed to avoid the braindye by using my magnifying glass and her timer."

Quincy was focused on carefully lowering their two captive teenagers. Once they were on the ground, she helped them undo the lassos around their feet.

"You," Wil growled, glaring at the cowgirl.

"I'm sorry." Quincy held up her hands. "I'm really, truly, sorry."

"I guess you're helping now, and that's something. But seriously, Alexander, why are you two always convinced I need to be saved?"

Alexander shrugged, shoving his hands in his wet short pockets. "Well, technically you *were* being held in a cell at Fathoms of Fun."

"I guess that's true. But I could have gotten out."

"Sure." Alexander didn't agree, but he didn't want to argue. Theo definitely would have wanted to. "And then you were acting like a vampire."

"I was not!"

"Well, *we* thought you were. And in our defense, you never tell us anything. If you would just talk to us, we'd know you were planning on sneaking back into a water park at night, or were staying up late to use the Wi-Fi, not because you were vampirically averse to the sun, *and* we'd have known you and Edgar were faking. But how did you two avoid getting braindyed?"

Edgar patted where his breast pocket would be in his suit jacket, then let out a small, disgusted noise upon discovering he was still wearing a tie-dyed shirt and not a suit at all. "The glasses were mine; the fake Mrs. Widow used them without permission to hide her eye color from us. Perhaps Theo suspected they were from someone nefarious because of that association! But we couldn't risk being clearer in the note, in case someone else saw it first. Anyhow, I had the glasses, and I put them on to shield my eyes from the garish colors in the dyeing room. Because of the tint, I discovered the subliminal messages. Once you realize what someone's trying to force on you, it's easier to resist."

"So you wore the glasses, too?" Quincy asked Wil.

"Nope, I went in first. I'm a genius, though, so it didn't affect me."

Quincy laughed like it was a joke, but Alexander didn't. He wasn't surprised. Well, maybe a little. He knew Wil was smart, but he'd always sort of taken it for granted. Wil was just Wil.

"Oh, you're— Really?" Quincy tried to adjust her cowgirl hat in an embarrassed fidget, but she wasn't wearing one.

"Yes." Wil stated it like a simple fact. "My brain processes information faster and on more levels than most people, so I was able to separate everything I was seeing and hearing into individual parts. Which I immediately put together with what I had read about Camp Creek on Gulp—it has excellent reviews, all from parents raving about how happy and normal their children were after attending, which made me suspicious, because all the reviews sounded exactly the same. No two kids are the same, so how would they all be having exactly the same experience? Unless someone was forcing them to, of course. Adults are always trying to tell kids how to behave, how to feel, how to think. I've never been good at listening to that."

"So you and Edgar were faking to get access to the whole camp," Alexander said. "You could have included Theo and me!"

"Technically, you were a mindless child drone."

Alexander frowned, trying not to be hurt. "Well, yeah. But you gave up your phone. And it says in Mom's letter that you're supposed to use it! I think this camp tried to take away the things that make us ourselves. For me, it was my caution. They made me so I wasn't worried about anything." Alexander wouldn't mind a little bit of that, but they had gone way too far. "And they probably would have made Theo boring and a rule follower. And they made you give up your phone."

"Like I would ever surrender Rodrigo." Wil retrieved Rodrigo from where it was hanging from a boondoggle hidden beneath her shirt. Finally, a boondoggle with a purpose. Rodrigo's familiar set of shiny stickers and glowing screen had never been such a welcome sight. "I gave them my burner phone."

"You have a burner phone?" Alexander had heard of burner phones but only in spy movies and things like that. Burner phones were untraceable phones, used to do things when you didn't want to be traced. Usually illegal things. Alexander's heart began racing. "Wil, are you an *evil* genius?"

She ruffled his hair the way he hated but liked when

she did it, because it meant she was paying attention to him. "I only use my powers for good. Now, come on. Let's go get Theo. Surely between the five of us, we can figure out where those books are hidden. Edgar and I have been all over this place with no luck. Other than the whole braindyeing scheme, this camp is exactly what it looks like on the surface."

"The surface." It made Alexander think of something, but he couldn't quite remember what. Then he snapped his fingers. "Giant ground sloths!"

"Is that some sort of camp cheer we don't know about?" Edgar asked. "Because I had to learn that whole terrible clapping game, and I can't get it out of my head."

"No! Theo was telling me that this area was populated with ancient giant ground sloths. They didn't live in trees. They dug massive tunnels instead. I'll bet there are still tunnels under the camp. I wonder if that's how those campers disappeared!"

"Right!" Quincy agreed.

"Campers disappeared?"

"In a book. We'll show you later. Our mom was in a photo! Twice. It's a confusing picture. But we're pretty sure one of Edgar's dads was here, along with Mina and

Lucy's dad, and Quincy's mom, and Edgaren't! And Dr. Jay! And our mom and Quincy's mom were some of the campers who disappeared."

"Tunnels, huh. That tracks. I'll bet that's where Edgaren't is, and where we'll find the books," Wil said.

"Why do you call him Edgaren't?" Quincy asked timidly.

"It's a long story," Alexander said. "A whole book, even."

"Whatever we call him, he's your uncle. Your uncle who stole my books," Wil said, her voice darker than the night around them. "And I want them back, Quincy Van Helsing."

"I'm not a Van Helsing," Quincy said. She sounded small and sad, nothing like her usual brash, rope-swinging self. "When my parents disappeared—"

"Your parents disappeared?" Edgar asked. "When?"

"I didn't know that," Alexander said softly, taking her hand and squeezing it.

Quincy sounded a little braver, squeezing Alexander's hand back. "At the beginning of the summer. I thought they were on an emergency work trip. My mom's job is super important and sometimes dangerous. But the next morning, my uncle showed up. He promised that he would help me, and that I could help all of you, and once we were—

well, once we were good and normal, then all our problems would be solved. I thought he meant he was going to find our parents. But I don't think that anymore. He dropped me off here and let me get braindyed. He never wanted to help me at all. He just wanted to change me."

"What's your last name?" Wil asked.

"Graves. Quincy Graves."

"Graves!" Wil shouted. "One of the seven families!"

Alexander didn't know what Wil was talking about, but then he remembered the secret library in the Sanguine Spa. "The old books that Edgaren't stole were in the photo, too. There was a Sinister book, and a Widow book"—Edgar raised his hand to claim that name—"and a Graves book. And your parents disappeared at the beginning of the summer, which was the same time my parents dropped us off at Aunt Saffronia's in the middle of the night."

Edgar sounded the same way Alexander felt—sad and worried. "And the same time my dads dropped me off at the water park in a suspicious hurry. They seemed . . . afraid."

"Come on," Wil said. "Let's go get Theo and find those tunnels. It's time to steal our books. After we have them, then we'll have a talk with Dr. Jay."

Alexander didn't want to go in any tunnels, and he didn't want to go back to camp. Things really had been simpler and easier when he was normal, when his brain had been dyed the same bright, simple colors as everyone around him.

But even though he didn't want to do these things, he knew he could. And he knew he had to. He wasn't going to let this camp decide what made a kid good or normal. There was no way he'd let Dr. Jay keep dyeing over the patterns that made kids themselves. Alexander was anxious, and introverted, and he didn't like group sports, and he refused to swim in lake water, and he could list ten dangers they'd face just on the walk back to get Theo. He was also funny, and clever, and empathetic, a good friend and brother, and an excellent cook. No one had the right to take any of that away from him.

"Let's do this," he said, taking a step toward the camp and immediately tripping over number seven on his list of dangers in the night: exposed roots. "I'm okay!" he shouted, jumping back up. "Watch for exposed roots!"

CHAPTER
TWENTY-EIGHT

Although she had flung out the idea of Guess My Sixth-Favorite Animal as a panicked last resort, Theo had to admit she was really into it now.

The campers and counselors had refined the rules. Other than eliminating animals not currently found somewhere on the planet, they couldn't ask any animal-specific questions. But they did ask a lot of other interesting questions to narrow down the types of things Theo liked, such as whether she'd rather live in the desert or the rain forest, where she'd go on vacation if she could go anywhere in the world besides Camp Creek (naturally all the counselors and campers agreed that Camp Creek was the ideal vacation), and which letter of the alphabet she found most appealing.

The whiteboard was covered in notes, the brackets being filled in with increasingly accurate and surprising options. Theo was so into it that she didn't notice the *pssts* being whispered at her with ever-louder volume until a rope snaked along the ground and snagged her foot. Theo looked over and saw Wil, Edgar, Quincy, and Alexander waiting in the dark next to a cabin. They gestured frantically.

"I, uh, have to use the bathroom!" Theo said, standing.

The counselors waved her away, everyone intently focused on the debate between whether it was better to have defensive body structure or be able to jump quickly, a real tortoise-versus-hare situation.

"But kangaroos—" Kiki started.

Georgie squeezed her shoulder. "Kiki! We've already eliminated kangaroos! Remember that Theo chose a bag over big pockets, so clearly she doesn't value attached pouches!"

"Right! How could I forget!" Kiki laughed at herself as Theo sidled away. "Let's talk turkey vultures!"

Theo joined the others in the darkness next to the

cabin. "That was fast!" she whispered. "How did you wash their brains that quickly?"

"My brain is and always has been my own, thank you very much." Wil grabbed Theo and hugged her. "Who did you think left you those glasses?"

"I— Well, I wasn't sure." Theo shrugged. "I assumed as soon as I saw you without Rodrigo, and Edgar in that awful outfit—"

Edgar sighed, the exhalation long and melancholy. Alexander loved the word *melancholy*. It was like sadness set to a melody, deeper and more elegant than plain old *unhappiness*. It suited Edgar perfectly. "It's not my fault," he said.

"I know! Exactly! I assumed neither of you would willingly be like this, so you must have been braindyed."

Wil tapped her foot impatiently. She put her hand against her chest, where Theo could see the outline of Rodrigo now that she was close. It must have been taking all Wil's willpower to leave her phone hidden. "Everyone here is in control of their own brains. But Edgar and I haven't found anything. We think what we're looking for must be under the camp."

"Ancient ground sloth tunnels," Alexander said, nudging Theo happily.

"Oh my gosh, you're right! They were all over this region! So cool and creepy. Imagine their claws."

Alexander shuddered. "I am. So where do we go?"

"That's just it." Wil sounded cross. "I don't know. We've been all over every inch of this place and haven't seen anything that looked like it might lead to a tunnel. And I couldn't find any schematics online. So unless we wander around, hoping one of us falls in a hole and disappears . . ."

"Holes. Holes." Theo tapped her forehead. "Disappearing! Henry!"

"Are we sure Theo hasn't been braindyed?" Edgar peered at her, worried.

"No! There's a boy here named Henry. He hides under the cabins. But twice now he's disappeared on me. He must be going in tunnels!"

"So we should crawl around under the cabins?" Alexander tried not to sound as terrified as he was, but he definitely didn't want to do that. Tunnels were bad enough. Crawl spaces? He'd had enough of those at the Sanguine Spa. And at least that had been in walls. Not under entire buildings with all that weight looming above you, waiting to squash you like a slug.

"No, we don't have time. And I can't imagine Dr. Jay

or Edgaren't scooting on their bellies in the dirt to get to a tunnel." Theo paced. "Oh! The office closet!"

"We checked the closet," Wil said, impatient. "We left a window open to snoop, but someone closed it."

"That was you? I mean that was me! Who closed it. Sorry."

"I'll bet we almost caught each other," Edgar said. "We did want to involve you, but they were always watching."

"And I wanted to keep you out of trouble," Wil added.

"Good job on that one!" Theo laughed. "But no, not in the closet. *Under* the closet. That part beneath the building had a concrete foundation, which didn't make structural sense. I'll bet anything it's actually stairs going down into the tunnels."

"I hope you're right," Edgar said. "Because we're betting a lot on it."

"Come on!" Theo led them to the office. She shimmied through the window, helping haul Alexander in. Quincy lassoed the far doorknob and used her rope to climb up, and Wil and Edgar used their teenager-long legs to climb in. Theo hurried to the closet door and picked the lock.

"When did you learn to do that?" Alexander asked as Quincy made an approving noise.

Theo had been right—it was much better with an

audience to impress. "It's amazing what you can learn when you're avoiding group activities." Theo popped the door open, and they all knelt down to examine the floor.

"Look!" Quincy pointed at hinges in a couple of the floorboards, so small they were impossible to notice if you weren't looking for them. There was a tiny knothole in the wood. Theo stuck her finger through and pried up the floor. It revealed narrow, steep concrete steps that went straight down.

"No handrail," Alexander said with a sigh.

"And no lights," Quincy added.

"No problem." Wil whipped out Rodrigo, turning on the flashlight. They all crept down the stairs, wondering what they would find in the darkness beneath the camp.

But they should have been more worried about what would find *them* in the darkness.

CHAPTER

TWENTY-NINE

"There's not a guide in that book?" Wil asked, looking up and down the surrounding dark tunnels. They were at an intersection and had no idea which way to go. The longer they took, the more likely it was they would be found before they could do any finding.

Theo shoved the book toward Wil, frustrated. "No, like I already told you, it doesn't have a map of secret tunnels beneath the camp. Quincy flipped through every page."

"We can't possibly explore the whole tunnel network in time." Alexander was tired of tunnels. Why did everywhere they go have tunnels? And this camp didn't even have a library like the water park and the spa. "Camp Creep, more like," he muttered to himself, his mood worsening. Just this morning, he had been in the sunshine, playing and having a great time, and now he was in the dark under the earth, miserable and stressed out.

He didn't want to go back to this morning—he didn't—but he was upset that this was the alternative.

Theo was mad, too. She had felt so triumphant finding the way into the tunnels, but now they were lost and everyone was disappointed in her. She was tired of being responsible. She'd taken on a lot of responsibility since they arrived at camp. Just this morning, she had been in the sunshine, pretending to play and faking having a great time, and now she was in the dark under the earth, miserable and stressed out.

Quincy was trying to be helpful, probably to make up for her previous betrayal. "I could run down this tunnel as fast as I can go. If we each take one tunnel—"

"No splitting up," Edgar said firmly. "I—"

Wil looked down at her phone. "What?" she gasped. "No. No, no, no."

"What?"

"I had my phone on silent so no one would notice it. I missed a text from Mina. She and Lucy are on their way *here*. They got a special invitation to the camp. And I don't have reception in these wretched tunnels, so I can't text them back and warn them. If we don't find what we need and figure this all out . . ."

"Then Mina and Lucy are going to get braindyed." Alexander didn't want that to happen. He liked Mina exactly how she was. *Like* liked her, even, though he would never admit it. "And Lucy definitely can't do group activities out in the sunshine!"

Theo stomped her foot. "What good are these tunnels anyway, unless we just want to hide!"

"What?" a voice called from the darkness.

"What?" five voices called back.

"You're the one who shouted for me." Henry skulked out of one of the tunnels, still filthy, his face a sullen frown. Theo had never been able to get a good look at him, but now that he was illuminated by Rodrigo, she saw he had a sour, unpleasant sort of face. Like he had just been told he was having beet salad for dinner.

"Henry!" she said. "Thank goodness. We need you to show us around the tunnels, and fast."

He shoved his hands in his pockets. "No."

"What?" Theo couldn't believe it. "But we need your help."

"So? I've needed help, too, and no one was around to help me. I had to find these tunnels and figure out how to hide from my aunt, how to sneak food and scrounge for clothes and blankets, how to steal from my own dad's camp. It's been scary and lonely and hard ever since he left, and no one! Not one person! Has helped *me*!" His voice raised to a yelling pitch, his face going dark with emotion.

Alexander stepped forward, his own voice soft. "I'm so sorry. That does sound really hard and scary. I can't imagine how I would have gotten through this summer without my sisters. What's your name?"

"Henry. Hide."

"We're not going to hide!" Theo snapped. "We're going to figure this out, with or without your help."

Henry's eyes bulged with anger. "No, Hyde. My name is Henry Hyde. H-Y-D-E."

"The Hyde book!" Wil crowed. "That's one of the books Edgaren't put in his trunk and stole!"

Alexander couldn't believe it. What were the odds? "Wait, Theo. Show him the photo."

She got out the book and flipped to the photo page. Henry frowned down at it. "That's my dad," he said, pointing to the scowling young man.

"Your dad—" Alexander said.

"Did he—" Wil continued.

"Disappear—" Edgar said.

"At the beginning of the summer?" Quincy finished in a rush.

Henry glared suspiciously. "How did you know?"

"Because all of ours did, too." Theo sighed. "And let me guess, you'd never met your aunt before then."

Henry shook his head.

"We're in this together," Theo said. "All of us. Whatever's going on, it has to do with our families."

Henry took a step back. His breathing was harsh and fast, and Theo didn't know whether he was angry or scared. Maybe he didn't know, either. Theo often had a hard time figuring out what she was feeling, too.

"No," Henry said, "I'm on my own! I've been fine on my own. Hiding keeps me safe, and I don't need any of you messing that up. Get out of here. This is *my* hiding spot, *my* way to stay safe!"

"I understand more about being scared now," Theo said, putting a hand on Henry's shoulder. "I *hate* being scared. But it's okay to feel that way sometimes."

Alexander stepped closer, too. "Sometimes being scared helps us know what's important to us. Like, I'm scared of getting sick or hurt, because I don't want to inconvenience anyone. And I'm scared of the people I love getting sick or hurt, because I don't want them to be in pain. So I'm always watching out for ways that bad things might happen. I'm extremely cautious. Being safe is important to me, too. But hiding isn't the same thing as being safe."

"You shouldn't have to be alone in the dark," Quincy added. "And you shouldn't let selfish people force you to be someone you aren't. It's not the same as being brain-dyed, but it's still changing because of them. Letting them turn you into someone who is a bad friend," she said.

"Or someone who participates in group games and swims in lakes," Alexander said, shuddering.

"Or someone who wears tie-dye," Edgar said, once again picking mournfully at the hem of his shirt.

"I can't promise you safety," Wil said, "but I can promise you I'll do whatever I can to take down anything standing between us and our parents. Because I'm sure of one thing now: if they could get back to us, they would. So we're going to get back to them instead. Together."

Henry scowled, then let out a low growl. "Fine. You said your books are inside a trunk? I'll take you."

Henry disappeared down a tunnel. Alexander reached out, and even in the dark, Theo's hand found his as they followed.

CHAPTER
THIRTY

"Is that it?" Henry sullenly pointed at a trunk sitting in the intersection between several more tunnels.

"That's it," Quincy said. "That's his trunk."

"Definitely. We had to carry it up a bunch of stairs." Theo glared at it.

Wil tugged on the lid, then huffed in frustration. "It's locked," she said, pointing at a huge lock hanging off the clasp, taunting them all.

Theo took a deep, satisfied breath. She reached into her pocket to pull out her tools. "I can pick it. Just give me—"

Henry roared forward, a huge rock in his hands. He brought it down with a crash once, twice, three times.

The lock was still intact, but the clasp wasn't. It hung askew, totally disconnected from the lid.

"Got it unlocked," Henry said, chest heaving.

Quincy patted his shoulder. "Good job."

Wil flipped open the trunk. "Those monsters," she gasped. Everyone else raced forward to see what Wil was so upset about. On top of the stacked books and a bunch of clothing and personal items too big to fit in the locked office desk drawers was a collection of cell phones, probably belonging to every single counselor here and some of the campers as well.

Quincy grabbed her cowgirl hat and settled it on top of her head with a happy sigh.

"The books," Alexander prodded.

"Right." Wil snatched her burner phone—identical to the real Rodrigo, cleverly disguised with the same stickers—and handed Edgar his own phone.

Edgar reached in and pulled out his suit. "The least they could have done was hang it," he grumbled, smoothing out the wrinkles. "No respect for style or class. Though I shouldn't have expected anything else from someone who forces everyone to wear tie-dye whether it flatters them or not."

"You always look cute," Wil mumbled, then froze,

blushing furiously. She grabbed the books and began shoving them toward waiting arms.

"Why is my book locked?" Henry demanded.

"They're all locked," Quincy answered. "See?" She waved the Graves book in front of him.

"I'll pick them! I know I can do it." Theo cracked her knuckles. But the locks were small. Too small for her current tools. "Drat," she muttered. "I need better tools. Let's—"

"We solved it!" a chipper voice behind them said. The six rule breakers slowly turned around to find their way to the surface blocked by a dozen camp counselors, shoulder to tie-dyed shoulder, uniform smiles on their faces.

"Solved what?" Wil asked. "Where we were?"

"No, silly! What Theo's sixth-favorite animal is!"

"Doubtful," Theo said, snorting a laugh. She hadn't figured out Lucy's, and there was no way this goofy bunch of braindyed teenagers had—

"Pangolin!" Kiki declared.

Theo's jaw dropped. "That's— You— Yeah. Yeah. That's it. You figured it out. You won." She numbly took the book that Wil was insistently holding out, barely feeling it in her fingers. "You really won. Wow."

"Look what we can accomplish when we all work together!" Heidi said.

"When everyone is in sync, and happy, and normal!" Ricky beamed at them.

"When everyone is doing what they're supposed to, and not running around in mysterious tunnels beneath the camp!" Kiki took a step forward. "I'm afraid you'll have to come back with us now! Dr. Jay told us that if anyone breaks rules, they need to be sent to the tie-dye cabin immediately! And I'm sorry to say that the three of you campers missed curfew and a really fun toothbrushing session! And that you two counselors were not following the schedule! And that you—" She tilted her head, trying to figure out who filthy Henry Hyde was. "Oh! I won Spot the Skulker! One million points for everyone! Don't worry, I'm sure she'll take care of you, too!"

All the counselors took a step forward as one. There was no way around them, no way to stop them.

"We can fight our way out." Henry gripped his book like he was ready to hit someone with it.

"It's not their fault they're like this." Alexander remembered what it had felt like, how easy it was. How deep the dye had soaked. It had taken a lot to break him out of it, to remind him of the things that made him himself.

Henry took a menacing step forward. "They've been going to the tie-dye cabin for three weeks now! You'll never be able to snap them out of it."

"We need something stronger than the braindye," Theo said, looking at Alexander. "Something that can wash it away. Something even more powerful than Dr. Jay's messages."

Wil's phone chimed, and she held it up, searching for reception. All the counselors froze, their eyes going to Rodrigo with the same inescapable magnetism that Wil's did.

"Pavlov's bell," Alexander whispered. "Wil! Play every text notification chime there is!"

"What?" Wil clutched Rodrigo possessively.

"Just do it!"

Wil looked annoyed, but she scrolled through the options and played each one. With every ding, chime, and whistle, the counselors' smiles dropped, their uniform posture changing and shifting. Until Wil hit one that sounded like an old phone ringing, and they all flinched away as one.

"Yeah, no, that's terrible, I hate it when people call me," Wil muttered. She went back to the text notification sounds.

"I—I don't think I like wearing shorts," Heidi said, staring down.

Theo pointed. "She didn't speak with an exclamation mark! It's working!"

"I hate ponytails," Kiki said, reaching up. "This isn't even my hair." She pulled off a wig to reveal a super-cool buzz cut, dyed bright pink.

"I wanted to go to LARPing camp." Ricky slouched and glared at everyone around him. "I didn't want to live-action role-play as a camp counselor. They don't even use weapons."

"Look at how gross my nails are from all that clay!" Georgie shrieked, her exclamation mark not a happy one as she held out her hands, examining them.

"The last touch," Theo said. She and Alexander tipped over the trunk. All the confiscated phones came tumbling out. With cries of happiness and horror mixed together, all the counselors dove for their phones, unable to look at or care about anything else.

"You know what," Wil said, staring down, "that's actually kind of creepy. I need to spend less time on my phone." She slipped Rodrigo into her pocket.

"And we need to get out of here while we can." Alexander pointed, the way through clear once more. They eased past the screen-lit teenagers and raced for the stairway that would lead them back to the office.

Alexander was first up it, but he froze with his hands pressed against the trapdoor.

"Why did we stop?" Quincy asked. Alexander shushed her, holding up a finger over his mouth. Because above them in the office he heard the angry voice of Dr. Jay and an all-too-familiar voice coming out of a mouth that was half-covered with a large, mean mustache.

"Edgaren't is here," he whispered, his stomach dropping in dread.

CHAPTER
THIRTY-ONE

Edgaren't sounded extremely angry. "What do you mean you didn't search their pockets? If the things we need weren't in their luggage, they've got to be in their pockets. It's not enough to have the books. You know that. We can't even get them open yet." That was a relief, at least.

But it was hard to feel too relieved, knowing all that separated them from Edgaren't was a flimsy trapdoor in a closet.

Dr. Jay answered. She had dropped her soothing voice. She spoke now in a thin, strained tone, like a rubber band stretched so far it could snap at any moment. "Don't lecture me! I know as well as you do what's at stake. She's my friend, too. But while you've been running around with your little plots, I've been hard at work here, perfecting my techniques! I care about these children, their future. We couldn't save the others, but we can save them still."

Who couldn't they save? Theo looked at Alexander, but he shrugged.

"If you care so much, then you should be helping me more. None of your work here will matter until we have everything we need. I'm going to get my trunk, and then we'll get the kids. And *I* won't let anything slip by."

Alexander gestured frantically for the others to go back down the stairs. "He's coming!" he hissed.

"We need another way out, and fast." Theo turned to Henry. She was holding the Siren book and the disguised camp book, while Alexander clutched the Blood and Stein books. Quincy had the Graves book, Henry the Hyde book, Edgar the Widow book, and Wil the Sinister book. None of them wanted to lose the books or to be found by the man with the small, mean eyes, large, mean mustache, and extremely loud, mean steps coming toward the stairs.

"Follow me!" Henry booked it, which, in this case, meant went very fast while also carrying his book.

The others followed him, sprinting through the tangle of tunnels.

"Wait!" Theo stopped, and the others skidded to a stop, too, staring back at her impatiently. "Look."

Carved on the wall were initials. She reached up and traced her mother's: *S.S.* Beneath it, with an arrow pointing down a long, dark corridor they weren't taking, was a sentence.

If you don't find me, I'll find you, it said.

"What if this is a message from her?" Theo asked.

Alexander shook his head. "But she was here as a teenager. She wouldn't have left a note for us then. Besides, we don't know if this note was from her or for her."

"He's going to catch up to us!" Quincy whispered from ahead of them.

Alexander stared into the inky blackness. He knew in a way he couldn't understand or explain that there would be answers in that direction. What answers to which questions, he couldn't say. "The ones who disappeared," he whispered. Did they go this way? Was this a clue?

"We have to go!" Henry hissed. Theo grabbed Alexander's hand and tugged him away from the carving in the wall. Several passages later, in a small side tunnel, there was an old ladder propped against the wall. "Up here," Henry said. "It'll be a tight fit."

He handed his book to Quincy and climbed, squeezing through a black hole. Then he lowered his arms. They passed up the books one by one before following. A painfully tight squeeze led through a crack in some rocks and into a clearing surrounded by trees. In the distance, they could see the bonfire, but they were far enough away that they couldn't hear the other campers or counselors. There were no cabins nearby.

"We should be safe out here for a while," Henry said. "No one comes to this part of the woods, because it's never on the schedule. I like it, though. My dad liked it, too. He used to come out here when he was too upset and needed to do some screaming." Henry's face was dark, his chest heaving with breaths. "When he was too angry. Like I am."

"Maybe don't do the screaming thing right now," Alexander said. "On account of how we don't want to be found." He looked longingly back at the crack in the rocks. He couldn't shake the feeling that they'd gone the wrong way.

"Here, try this," Theo said to Henry. She wrapped her arms around herself, squeezing tightly. "It helps me sometimes."

Henry scowled dubiously, but he tried it. Gradually his face drained of some of the excess of blood and anger. He took deep breaths, then nodded.

"What do we do?" Quincy asked. "I don't want to go back with Uncle Van Helsing. I don't like the person he tried to make me."

"And I'm not about to let my terrible aunt get me in her clutches. I'll be mad whenever I feel like it!" Henry stomped to emphasize his point.

"We're not letting them take either of you," Theo said.

"And we're not letting them get these books." Wil was clutching the Sinister book to her chest like it was a baby. A large, book-shaped baby, with mysterious insides. Then again, if it were a normal baby, its insides would still be mysterious. And also not locked up.

She pulled out the keys—also around a boondoggle under her shirt—and set her book on the ground. "Why are there so many keys?" she muttered, flipping through them, trying to find the right one by looking at them.

"We don't have time for that," Theo said.

"Call Aunt Saffronia," Alexander said. "Have her pick us up."

Wil huffed an aggravated breath but reached into her pocket. She let out a heartbroken cry. "Rodrigo's battery is dead," she wailed. "I'm so sorry, Rodrigo. I failed you. I failed us all."

Theo and Alexander shared a long-suffering look. "We can bring Rodrigo back from the dead. All it takes is a little electricity. But in the meantime, we need a phone."

"Here!" Edgar grabbed Wil's burner and handed it over. "But we don't have your aunt's phone number programmed into this one. Or Mina's, so we can't warn her. How are we going to get to her before Edgaren't does?"

"That's okay," Alexander said. "I have Aunt Saffronia's number memorized. It's easy to remember because it's like a date. Month, day, year, like you'd find on a—" Alexander froze.

"Did someone break him?" Henry peered closer, waving a hand in front of Alexander's face. "Is he still brain-dyed? They freeze like this when they hear that terrible broadcast."

"No, the sound's not playing. It's something else." Theo grabbed Alexander's cheeks, turning his face to hers. The look on his face was scaring her, and she didn't like it. "What?"

"Do you remember our scavenger hunt in the cemetery last summer?"

"Yeah, of course. It was awesome. But this really isn't the time to reminisce."

"What's that mean?" Henry asked.

Theo answered without looking away from Alexander. Maybe he really was still braindyed. "*Reminiscing* is remembering something fondly. Like *remind* and *sense* put together, reminding yourself of the senses you had during an important time in your past. Alexander, I know you love scavenger hunts, but it isn't important right now. We can talk about it later."

"No, it is important. It's very important. Wil added the birth dates and death dates in her head to find the coordinates we needed. You guided us through the cemetery with your sense of direction. And I made up stories to go with the names on the headstones." Alexander tried to swallow, but his throat didn't want to cooperate. "Theo, Wil . . . I remember now why Aunt Saffronia's name was familiar, why her phone number was so easy to remember. It wasn't because I'd heard Mom talking about her. It was because I'd made up a story about her. While looking at her headstone in the family cemetery."

"What are you saying?" Theo demanded.

"I think—I think Aunt Saffronia's *dead*."

CHAPTER
THIRTY-TWO

Theo held up her hands. "Wait, wait. Wait. You're saying you think Aunt Saffronia—the aunt who has been driving us from place to place, the aunt whose house we stayed at, the aunt our parents left us with—is, what, a ghost?"

"Yes," Alexander said, his voice coming out a tortured squeak.

Wil looked from one twin to the other. "You two didn't know?"

"What?" Theo shrieked, aghast, because ghosts are always a surprise. "It's true? She's a ghost? We've been being taken care of by our dead aunt this whole time? And you *did* know?"

Wil shrugged, staring mournfully at Rodrigo's lifeless screen. "I really thought you two knew. I mean, she's pretty transparent. Both in the sense of being honest about it and in the sense of being literally transparent when the light hits her right. Didn't you think it was weird how she'd disappear? And reappear right when we needed her? And always said things like *when your parents summoned me* instead of when they called or texted or whatever?"

"Well, yeah. Of course we thought that was weird," Theo said.

"But we didn't immediately jump to *oh, she must be a ghost.*" Alexander began pacing, clutching the books he held to his chest like a shield. The phone in his hand felt like a threat now, the only way to connect to the great beyond and his aunt who dwelled there. "*Aunt Saffronia is a ghost.*"

"Charlotte is, too. And her sisters." Edgar seemed to take this in stride.

"Wait—the lifeguards? The identical lifeguards?" Theo sat down on the ground, so overwhelmed she couldn't stand anymore.

"You mean there weren't even real lifeguards at Fathoms of Fun?" This was somehow even more shocking and horrifying to Alexander than the fact that he now knew not one but several ghosts.

"There are real lifeguards now! But when Edgaren't and my aunt's terrible sister were running the park, they fired all the real lifeguards. Charlotte and her sisters stepped in to help. They're anchored to the park."

"She did say they'd always been welcome there," Theo said. Even her bees were quiet, stunned into stillness. "And that Edgaren't wanted them gone."

"Well?" Quincy said. "Are you calling your aunt, or not?"

"But she's *dead*," Alexander said.

"But she has a car?" Henry was getting angry again. "I don't care if she's a ghost or a vampire or a zombie or whatever, as long as she has a car and can get us away from here with our brains intact."

"A zombie definitely wouldn't get us away from here with our brains intact. Trust me," Quincy offered unhelpfully. Then, seeing the looks of horror on her friends' faces, she hurried on. "But ghosts don't eat brains! That I know of. I don't actually know a lot about ghosts. Sorry."

Wil drew Alexander and Theo aside. "I'm sorry," she said. "I guess I haven't been good about talking to you two. But Aunt Saffronia is a Sinister. We can trust her. She's bound to our family; she'll always help when summoned. I've been researching it, and Charlotte told me some things, too. Only our family can call her or dismiss her, but there are some places it's harder for her to be. That's why she couldn't come here. Ghosts need an anchor to a place or an object, but they also need belief and weirdness to welcome them. And Camp Creek—"

"Isn't big on weirdness," Theo finished. "You should call her, Alexander. Ghost or not, she's family."

Alexander nodded. His head was spinning. He didn't understand what this summer had turned his world into. But they needed to get out, and fast. It helped that Wil had taken the books Alexander was holding, leaving Theo free to take his empty hand in hers. She squeezed, and he dialed Aunt Saffronia's number.

Also known as her date of death.

This time the ringing echoing through a vast tunnel of static made more sense. Aunt Saffronia answered, sounding like mist looked: solid until you got closer, when it just disappeared. As long as Alexander wasn't paying too much attention, Aunt Saffronia's voice sounded like a voice. But now that he was listening—really listening—it wasn't a voice so much as the impression of a voice. The memory of one.

"You summoned me?" Aunt Saffronia said.

"What are we supposed to find here?" Alexander asked. He knew Aunt Saffronia wouldn't come pick them up until they found what she wanted them to—Theo's timer at the water park, and Alexander's magnifying glass at the spa. They had sort of found the books here, or at least found them again. Hopefully that was enough. He couldn't stand the idea of her telling him to look closer, or that they needed more time, or some other vague hint that would send them back into the camp in a desperate search.

"There is nothing at that dreadful place for you. Only danger. All you need to do is get out. I cannot come help you, because—" She paused, and the static grew louder, like she was standing in a windy tunnel. "I cannot come at all," she said, her voice dropping to a whisper that still felt like a scream in Alexander's ear. "Something is pulling me away. Something is stopping me. Dear child, whatever you do next, you must not go to—"

And then the line went as dead as Aunt Saffronia apparently was.

Alexander looked up at the others to tell them what had happened, but he looked past his friends instead. Right at Edgaren't and Dr. Jay, standing behind Wil and Edgar.

Edgaren't was holding a phone. He smiled, a smile like a punch in the stomach, a smile that made his small, mean eyes smaller and meaner, and his large, mean mustache as large and mean as it ever was. "Thanks," he said to whoever was on the other end of the line. "I think that took care of her." He hung up and put his phone in his pocket. "Things that can be summoned can also be sent away. Remember that. It will be important later."

"But only by family," Wil said. "Charlotte told me!"

"Which means someone in our family is . . . helping him?" Theo felt anger buzzing to life in her. Anger that would put Henry's to shame. "Who's helping you?"

"I'll be taking those now," he said, ignoring her question as he snatched the keys from her. "Along with the books and whatever else you've stolen. Then we're going to go back to camp, together. No one is coming to help you."

Wil grabbed the Sinister book before Edgaren't could. Then she, Quincy, Henry, and Edgar all scurried across the forest clearing to stand side by side with Theo and Alexander. Theo's hand tightened in his. Everyone held their books to their chests like armor. But it didn't matter. Edgaren't had the keys, and anyway, he was right: They were on their own. No one was coming to save them.

Edgaren't had finally gotten them exactly where he wanted them.

CHAPTER
THIRTY-THREE

"We're not going with you!" Alexander shouted, surprising himself. But he was in a fragile emotional state right now. There had been the braindyeing, then coming back to himself, then the tunnels and the books, and now finding out Aunt Saffronia not only wasn't coming but also had been a ghost the whole time. It was a lot to deal with.

"Whyever not?" Dr. Jay peered at him, tilting her head. Her voice was back to the soft, soothing tones she used in the tie-dye cabin of doom.

"Because you're evil!"

"I'm evil?" Dr. Jay blinked, her bland face barely making any expression at all. "I saw you out there, at camp.

You and Quincy both. You were having so much fun. Weren't you?"

"Not on purpose!" Alexander glared at her.

"But does it matter *why* you were having fun? The point is, you and Quincy were part of a group. You were enjoying healthy activities. You were doing exactly what you should be doing at your age. And, Theo, didn't it upset you that you couldn't enjoy all the fun the way the others were? Didn't you feel left out?"

"No!" Theo said, but it was a lie. She definitely had felt left out, and stressed out, and put out. Lots of outs.

Alexander, too, had to admit that Dr. Jay was right. He'd been part of a group, more so than he'd ever been in his whole life. And even though he was doing things he'd never choose to, hadn't it been easy? It hadn't been scary or stressful. No one had laughed at him, or excluded him, or been annoyed with him when he wouldn't or couldn't do what they wanted him to.

But it hadn't really been *him* they liked. In fact, he couldn't think of the names or faces of a single other kid in their cabin or even in the whole camp. They were all a tie-dyed blur of smiles and group activities. No one stood out. No one was an individual. No one was a real friend, because no one was themselves.

"I might have been having fun," he said, "but it wasn't my choice. I should get to choose *how* I have fun. And yeah, maybe sometimes that's participating in games. But sometimes that's finding a good book and curling up to read while cheering on Theo and our friends. And that's okay, too. That doesn't mean I'm not having a good childhood or that I'm defective."

"Yeah," Theo said, stomping her foot in agreement. "Just because I *could* have had fun doing these camp activities doesn't mean someone should force me to. I should have been able to have fun on my own terms. And boondoggles are stupid!"

Dr. Jay gasped, her hand going to the boondoggle key chain at her waist. "You take that back," she whispered.

"You tried to tell me how I should and shouldn't feel!" Henry shouted, his voice punching through the night like an angry fist. "But I feel the way I feel! My dad understood! He helped me deal with my feelings instead of pretending like they didn't exist! He never treated me like an inconvenience or like there was something wrong with me because I wasn't happy all the time! You aren't helping the campers. You're making them into pretend versions of real kids."

"Your father was—" Dr. Jay shouted, her own face

going red. She cut herself off, taking a deep breath. Then she sniffed, her nose wrinkling like the skin on oatmeal left out too long. "You're all just like your parents."

"How did you know them?" Theo demanded.

"Where did they disappear to back then?" Alexander asked.

"And where are they now?" Wil demanded.

Dr. Jay shook her head. "That's none of your business. My past is my past, but *your* futures are my responsibility. I couldn't save them back then. I tried. We all did. But I can save you. I know what's best for you, whether you like it or not."

"You don't know *us*, though," Quincy said. "So how can you know what's best for us?"

"Because I know what's best for every child, and it's the same thing! If everyone will behave how I tell them to, then I'll be perfectly happy!"

Alexander frowned. "Don't you mean *they'll* be perfectly happy?"

Dr. Jay stumbled over her words, tumbling them out as fast as she could to correct her misstep. "Yes, obviously. That's what I mean. This is for the children."

"Sounds like it's for you," Wil said with a dismissive eye roll. There was nothing quite so wounding as getting a dismissive eye roll from a cool teenager. No adult was immune. Dr. Jay put a hand over her heart.

"Nonsense!" she snapped. "This is all nonsense, and I don't have to listen to any of you, because you're children and I'm an adult and therefore I know everything and you know nothing. Now. Let's get you all back to the tie-dye cabin and fix you right up."

"We're not moving without answers." Theo braced herself, ready to fight.

Dr. Jay lunged in a lightning-fast swirl of tie-dye. She grabbed the top book in the stack Wil was clutching. Wil cried out in anger as Dr. Jay held it up in triumph.

"I've got it! I've got . . . *Adventures in Advertising?* These aren't the books we need!" She turned in anger toward Edgaren't. "Are you betraying me, after all these years? You replaced the real books with my old textbooks?"

Alexander used their distraction to dial another number he had memorized. He held the phone to his ear, listening to it ring. At last, someone answered, snapping "What?"

Alexander hurriedly whispered information, then hung up before Edgaren't turned back to them again.

Edgaren't pointed to the rest of the books. "Those *are* the books. We've worked toward this for more than twenty years. I'm not going to stop." He loomed, taking a step closer to the children. "Give me those books, and everything else you're hiding."

"And then what?" Theo asked. "What are you going to do with us? The same thing you did with our parents?"

Edgaren't shrugged his massive shoulders. "I don't know where your parents are, either."

"What?" Alexander gasped.

"Liar!" Theo shouted. That couldn't be possible. Now that they knew Edgaren't was connected to all the missing parents, surely that was the explanation. He'd done something with them for nefarious purposes. They had been kidnapped—or adultnapped—and that was the reason they were gone. The reason this summer had been so sinister.

"Believe me, I've tried to find them. We all have."

Dr. Jay nodded. Her voice dropped back to that annoyingly soothing tone. "Does that hurt, knowing they left all of you on your own? Knowing that they didn't care enough to take you with them when they ran? We understand. We know exactly what that feels like. They left us behind, too. So you see, we care, little ones. We've always cared."

Henry let out a low growl. Theo's bees became an

angry swarm. And, for once, Alexander didn't know how to feel. Was that true? Did his mom and her friends leave some of their friends behind? Had they done it again, only this time to their own children?

"Don't worry," Edgaren't said. "I'm not going to do anything with you. Dr. Jay and I want the same thing we got for ourselves: for you all to be happy and normal. And if you don't do what we say, well. There's always the *other* camp."

Dr. Jay shuddered. "I didn't like it," she whispered. "But it was necessary."

"*A History of Summer Camps and the Unexplained Disappearances of Various Campers in the Mountainous Lake Regions*," Alexander whispered, his hand twitching in Theo's. "We're going to be the ones who disappear this time."

"Maybe," Theo said, looking nervously at Alexander. "Maybe we should give them the books. What choice do we have?"

Alexander dropped Wil's burner phone and clenched his free hand into a fist. "No. I'm not letting them take away my choices. Not again. If I want to be a weird kid who sits inside all summer and reads, then I will."

Quincy nodded. "And if I want to be a weird kid who

practices lassoing all day every day even though I can't get close enough to a real animal to ever use my lassoing skills for fun, then I will."

Henry let out a scream of primal rage that the others interpreted as him saying if he wanted to feel angry and deal with it in his own way rather than being forced to be happy all the time, then he would.

"And I'm never wearing this horrid cheap cotton again," Edgar said.

When she spoke, Wil's voice was so scary, Theo and Alexander didn't know how Edgaren't and Dr. Jay didn't cower before her. "And you're not taking Rodrigo *or* these books *or* my twerps of a brother and sister."

Edgaren't laughed. Each *ha* felt like someone pinching them, pulling their hair, whispering a nasty insult when the teacher wasn't looking. "And who's going to stop me?" he sneered.

There was a tremendous crashing noise, the cracks and snaps of underbrush being trampled as something huge and terrible came toward them from the trees.

"Giant ground sloth?" Theo gasped, wondering if they were about to be saved . . . or about to be eaten.

CHAPTER
THIRTY-FOUR

While a giant ground sloth would have been tremendously scary and exciting, *A History of Summer Camps and the Unexplained Disappearances of Various Campers in the Mountainous Lake Regions* had been correct in declaring them long-since extinct. But almost as terrifying as an aggressive, territorial, supersized sloth with insanely powerful claws was an aggressive, confused, hungry, and tired and no-longer-braindyed mass of teens and tweens.

Alexander had called the emergency office number and told them exactly where to find the grown-ups in charge.

"Oh no," Dr. Jay said as every single camper stampeded into the clearing. "I forgot to play the music, and no one visited the cabin today. It's all worn off! They're . . . they're . . . just kids again!" She took a step back, holding her hands in front of herself.

"I'm hungry!" the gap-toothed girl said, her hair already escaping its ponytail.

"I want to call my mom," a boy fighting back tears said. "I haven't talked to her all week, and I miss her, and you have to let me call her!"

"My bed is really uncomfortable," a girl said while tugging out her own ponytail and beginning to braid her hair. "Also, I have a lot of notes about the food here. I think the programming can be improved, too. What even is the point of making boondoggles?"

"I love boondoggles!" another kid shouted. "But I want to wear my own clothes! These shirts aren't washed well enough, and the dye keeps getting on my skin and making me look like I'm a zombie!"

"That's not how zombies look," Quincy said. "But your complaint is valid."

The other complaints began flying, fast and furious, a whole wall of them between Edgaren't and the Sinister-Winterbottoms and their friends. There was no way Dr.

Jay could braindye them again. She had officially lost control of Camp Creek.

"Go, now! While they're distracted!" Theo pointed, and they all followed her, sprinting through the trees.

"But the keys!" Wil cried out, casting an agonized look over her shoulder.

"Better to have the books and no keys than the keys and no books," Alexander said. Though it was terribly frustrating.

"There's a camp van!" Henry veered toward the office. "We used to use it to go on adventures and nature walks and library runs. It's parked by the gate, but we'll need the car keys from the office! I'm sick of keys!"

"I'll grab our things!" Quincy broke away toward Cabin Everything Good and Normal! Henry and the Sinister-Winterbottoms burst into the office and froze.

Kiki was sitting behind the desk. She had been such a stickler for the rules before. How were they going to get the car keys from her?

But Kiki wasn't Kiki anymore. Or rather, Kiki was finally Kiki again. She stared down at her phone, her boot-clad feet propped up on the desk, a giant bubble of gum the same shade as her hair extending from her purple-lipsticked lips.

"Where are the keys to the van?" Henry demanded.

Kiki shrugged, pointing at one of the desk drawers.

Theo darted there, ready to pick the lock, but Kiki hadn't bothered locking it. Unreasonably disappointed, Theo opened the drawer and grabbed a boondoggle key chain with dozens of keys attached to it. One of them had to be the right one. "We're stealing the van!" she said.

Kiki shrugged again. Her bubble gum bubble popped, and she sucked it back in, never taking her eyes off her phone. "Not my problem."

"Technically it belongs to my family, anyway!" Henry shouted. "So it's not really stealing! But I wouldn't care if it was!"

"Let's go." Wil held the door open. Quincy sprinted toward them, two suitcases, Wil's backpack, and Quincy's own duffel bag roped to her so she could carry them all at once. They shoved the family books into the extra space in Quincy's duffel bag and then ran down the road.

"What about your motorcycle?" Wil asked. Edgar's sparkly wheels had been moved, parked next to an enormous white van. "You look so cool on it."

"Sometimes it's more important to be practical than to look good. But only sometimes." Edgar threw open the sliding door to the van, and Henry Hyde, Quincy Graves, and Alexander and Theodora Sinister-Winterbottom climbed in. Sliding it shut, Edgar took the driver's seat. Wil took the passenger seat with a cry of relief at seeing a phone charger. She plugged in Rodrigo as Edgar started the van and peeled out.

Theo and Alexander peered out the back window as a child climbed the gate of Camp Creek and ripped down the K, replacing it with a boondoggle in the shape of a P.

"Camp Creep indeed." Alexander slumped, relieved to be getting farther and farther away from that terrible cabin and the terrible doctor who had tried to convince him the way he could be happiest was to be just like everyone else.

But also maybe a little sad that it hadn't worked. Because it really had been easy when he was braindyed. He had a feeling nothing on the road ahead of them would be easy at all. And he still couldn't shake the nagging worry that they had taken the wrong tunnel.

"So, what do we know?" Theo asked, still watching out the back window. She could have sworn she heard the rumble of an engine following them, but the road was twisty and dark, and she didn't see any signs of pursuit. "We have the books now, but Edgaren't has the keys. And we didn't get any real answers out of Dr. Jay."

"We know all our parents are missing," Quincy said.

Edgar nodded. "It can't be a coincidence. Or an accident. And we know they knew Edgaren't—I feel quite silly saying that, by the way—and Dr. Jay when they were younger."

"Do we believe Edgaren't that he doesn't know where they are?" Alexander asked, hoping the others would say they didn't. That surely Edgaren't was lying, and he had their parents.

Theo sighed. "He thought he was in control of us. So why would he lie about that?"

"He's looking for them, too," Wil said. "I'd bet anything on it. Which means we have to find them first. And figure out who banished Aunt Saffronia, and how, so we can get her back."

Theo tried to sound determined instead of frustrated. "We have the books now. I'll get those locks open as soon as I can find the right tools."

Wil nodded. "I'm sure there will be answers inside. And now we have Sinisters, Hydes, Graves, Widows, and—"

Edgar slammed on the brakes. There was a taxi on the road, coming straight toward them. Or toward Camp Creek, more likely. Edgar honked the horn and flashed his lights. The taxi stopped. Out climbed Mina, as pretty and sad-looking as ever with her big, dark hair and her big, dark eyes, and little Lucy, so blond and pale she almost glowed in the moonlight.

"Get in!" Edgar said. Theo threw the door open, and the sisters climbed inside.

"What's going on?" Mina asked.

Lucy said nothing, but she stared at Alexander with eyes that seemed to reflect the moonlight with an odd red glow. He waved nervously at her, and she smiled, still not showing the teeth he knew from a previous glimpse were shockingly fang-like.

"Edgaren't—" Theo said while Wil and Edgar said, "Heathcliff—" and Quincy said, "Van Helsing—"

"Is back there," Alexander finished. "And we know for certain now that our parents aren't gone for the summer. They're missing. Either Edgaren't was lying and he really did do something with them, or he was telling the truth and he hasn't been able to find them, either. It's up to us." He might not be braindyed anymore, but Alexander was different. He felt older than he had at the beginning of the summer. He was still cautious, but also braver, and more determined.

Theo, too, had changed. She was still brave, but she

understood a little more what it felt like to be scared, to wonder what other people were feeling, and to try to think and feel like they would, instead of barreling ahead with how she felt and what she wanted to do.

She was still brave, but she was also more cautious. And equally determined.

"We're going to find them. All of the parents," Theo declared.

"And figure out how to summon Aunt Saffronia again," Alexander added, because even though he was still quite upset that their aunt was a ghost, he didn't want her to be gone forever. They might need her again, and even if they didn't, she was family.

"Someone needs to tell me where we're headed," Edgar said.

"Well, we have all the families except two now," Wil said. "We're missing the Sirens and the Steins."

"The Steins!" Edgar snapped his fingers. "I just got some brochures for Stein Manor. It's a science camp."

"Not another camp," Quincy groaned.

"If it gets us answers," Alexander said, feeling very brave indeed, "then that's where we're going. Maybe by finding all the families from the books and pooling our information, we can figure out where our parents are, who Edgaren't is, what Dr. Jay knows about that long-ago summer our parents disappeared the first time, and what, exactly, is making *this* summer so sinister. The bad kind, not my family kind," he clarified.

"I like the family kind of Sinister," Quincy said, still sounding cautious and tentative.

Theo nudged her with her shoulder, grumbling as she said it but saying it nonetheless: "Our family kind of Sinister likes you, too."

"I hate this trip already," Henry grouched from the back of the van as Edgar started it back up and they set off down the road toward Stein Manor and whatever secrets—and hopefully answers—it held.

"Science camp could be fun," Wil said, looking at her siblings in the rearview mirror.

"Yeah, sounds electrifying," Theo answered with an eye roll, unaware of just how right she was.

Frankly, Stein Manor would be *very* electrifying indeed. . . .

ACKNOWLEDGMENTS

First, a confession: I love tie-dye. Love making it, love wearing it, love seeing it. Apologies to other tie-dye enthusiasts—we aren't *all* secretly trying to get kids to act the same as everyone else.

Second, not a confession: I still hate raisins.

But I still love my editor, Wendy Loggia; her assistant editor, Ali Romig; my agent, Michelle Wolfson; my publicist, Kristopher Kam; my publisher, Delacorte Press; my publisher's home, Random House Children's Books, and everyone that I have the privilege of working with there, especially my cover designer, Carol Ly, and my incredible cover artist, Hannah Peck. And special thanks to my copy editors, but also you're welcome: I'll never figure out how to use commas or dashes, and you'll always have job security.

Natalie Whipple still doesn't live next to me to share the yummy meals she makes, which seems rude, but she remains a bestie nonetheless. Stephanie Perkins lives even farther away, which is *definitely* rude—geography is a cruel mistress—but her love of the Sinister-Winterbottom twins and her willingness to vacation with them has helped me so much.

My parents let me be the nervous kid who took breaks from skiing or boating or otherwise adventuring in order to read, and I'll always be grateful to them for that.

I picked the person I wanted to go through life with when I was very young. Part of how I knew he'd be the best partner? He was more than happy to sit next to me on the couch, reading. I still love doing that with him, and I'm so glad we have three wonderful kids to join us. It's a full couch, but a good one.

And finally, my backyard dinosaur, Kimberly, still has not lifted so much as a claw to help me write any of these books, and would in fact eat me if I sat still long enough. But I love her as much as I hate raisins, so thanks. I'd rather have you than a hundred giant ground sloths. (Or even one giant ground sloth, for that matter, because: terrifying.)

ABOUT THE AUTHOR

Kiersten White has never been a lifeguard, camp counselor, or churro stand operator, and in fact has never once experienced summer or summer vacation or solved any mysteries during the aforementioned season. Anyone saying otherwise is lying, and you should absolutely not listen to them, even if they offer you a churro. *Especially* if they offer you a churro.

Though she was never a lifeguard, camp counselor, or churro stand operator, Kiersten is the *New York Times* bestselling author of more than twenty books, including *Beanstalker and Other Hilarious Scarytales*. She lives with her family near the beach and keeps all her secrets safely buried in her backyard, where they are guarded by a ferocious tortoise named Kimberly.

Visit her at kierstenwhite.com, or check out sinister summer.com for clues about what awaits the Sinister-Winterbottoms in their next adventures....

JOIN THE SINISTER-WINTERBOTTOM
TWINS IN THEIR NEXT ADVENTURE IN

SINISTER SUMMER

MENACING MANOR

CHAPTER ONE

The Sinister-Winterbottom children had no problems. Their summer was rolling along as merrily as a summer could, endless days and warm nights perfumed with sunscreen and bug spray, drenched in fun and relaxation.

Theo was well on her way to precisely calloused feet that allowed her to walk on hot pavement without feeling it. Alexander was well on his way to reading through an entire library's worth of mystery novels. Wil was well on her way to doing whatever sixteen-year-old sisters do on their phones all day, but doing it while lying out on a patio lounge chair instead of holed up in her bedroom. And they were all fueled by a steady supply of perfectly baked cookies and the occasional robot-battle break supplied by their parents.

Yes, nothing had gone wrong. No one was scared or worried. Their parents were exactly how parents should be during the summertime: there when you needed them for a meal or scraped knee or library run or movie night, and otherwise minding their own business as you minded your own absolutely delicious lack of business.

"No." Alexander sighed and opened his eyes. It was too absurd to imagine. If he was going to fantasize a different summer for them, he should have given Theo wings. She'd always wanted wings, while Alexander was happy to stay on the ground. There were more than enough things for him to worry about down here; he didn't want to have to start thinking of all the bad things that could happen if he added soaring through the skies to his daily activities. Territorial birds, flying through swarms of bees, collisions with drones, air sickness. See, there he was, already afraid of what could happen in a scenario he would literally never be in.

"No, what?" Theo asked. She was hunched over the pile of locked books. Seven books, to be exact, with seven family names on them. Each with a tiny, perfect, unpickable lock. But she *would* defeat these locks. When Theo set her mind to something, her focus and determination were fearsome to behold.

"I was trying to imagine us into a normal summer."

While Alexander was worried, Theo was mad. Along with Wil, they were crammed into a van with five new friends: Edgar Widow from Fathoms of Fun, Lucy and Mina Blood from the Sanguine Spa, Quincy Graves from Texas, and Henry Hyde from Camp Creek (who was only sort of their friend since he wasn't very friendly). The aggressively borrowed vehicle bumped and squeaked and grumbled down dark roads as they left Dr. Jay and her terrible braindyeing, and Edgaren't and his terrible Edgaren'tness behind.

They had also left the keys to these books behind, in the clutches of Edgaren't. It was all aggravating, which was a type of annoying that was so annoying it made you angry.

Theo imagined wings for herself, pictured soaring above the van, looping through the skies. Looking for threats and handily defeating them. She couldn't hold on to the fantasy, though, any more than Alexander could hold on to a dream of a normal summer.

"Yeah, no," she sighed, and went back to scratching at the locks with her tools from the ceramic building at

Camp Creek. There were two long, hooky metal things for scraping pots, and one narrow wooden stick thing for, well, she wasn't sure. The tools had worked great for picking door locks, and even drawer locks, but these book locks were itty bitty. There was no way her current tools would work, but Theo hated sitting still with nothing to do with her hands.

"Is it weird that I miss Aunt Saffronia's car?" Alexander asked. "When it wasn't disappearing around us, at least."

"I miss her house. When it actually had food for us, at least."

"I know we didn't know her well, and she's—" Alexander was about to say *a ghost*, but the words caught in his throat. The word *ghost* felt like he had swallowed a pancake with no butter or syrup on it, and it was stuck, sponged onto his insides, refusing to budge. Which was a terrible mental image. Both something being stuck in his throat, and a pancake without butter or syrup or whipped cream or jam or honey butter or apple butter or—

Alexander's stomach grumbled. "I miss the food, too," he said. He couldn't *believe* his last meal had been served buffet style. He missed Aunt Saffronia's clean kitchen, with its black-and-white tiles and marigold walls, where he could observe all the food-safety protocols.

He also missed the blissful innocence of not realizing their aunt Saffronia, who had been charged with taking care of them for the summer, was (a) dead, (b) had been dead the entire time, and (c) was somehow banished now, which meant she was . . . deader? Or still just as dead, but unable to reach them anymore? He wasn't certain of the logistics.

But he was certain that she had been the only grown-up person—well, person-*ish*—on their side. Now they didn't have anyone in charge of them, and Alexander really, really liked people being in charge. It made him feel safe and taken care of.

Theo didn't really like people being in charge of her, but she *did* really like knowing when she was going to have her next meal. And she liked weird Aunt Saffronia. It made her sad that someone had taken their aunt away from them, when their parents had very purposefully chosen Aunt Saffronia to take care of them.

Leaving Aunt Saffronia in charge seemed like a bizarre choice, made even bizarrier (Theo knew that wasn't a word, but felt like it should be: a combination of *more bizarre* and *scarier*) knowing that Aunt Saffronia was on the wrong side of the grave to be a good babysitter. But their parents had to have summoned Aunt Saffronia for a reason. They could have left Theo and Alexander with a neighbor. Or even with Wil, though to be fair even an occasionally incorporeal ghostly babysitter still paid more attention than Wil did.

Theo's aggressively borrowed wooden tool snapped in half. She set everything aside with a huff. She had to be careful or she'd jam the locks.

Mmm, jam. Without realizing it, her mind fell into the same hungry thought spiral as Alexander's as it snagged on jam, then peanut-butter-and-jam sandwiches, then peanut butter cookies. Though the Sinister-Winterbottom twins were very different, they still managed to land on the same thoughts frequently.